A Christmas Code

THE
CODE BREAKERS
SERIES

JACKI DELECKI

BESTSELLING AUTHOR

DEDICATION

To my lovely readers. My best wishes for Joy and Peace in the Holiday Season.

ACKNOWLEDGEMENTS

Thank you to my extraordinary team. Karuna, my plot partner, Valerie Susan Hayward, my amazing editor, and my always supportive husband. And to my support team who keep me writing. Maria Connor, Jen Rice, Cynthia Garlough, and my wonderous children. And to the outstanding Kim Killion, cover artist and Jennifer Jakes who make my books beautiful inside and out.

CHAPTER ONE

Hot and breathless from performing the newly imported French dance steps of the quadrille, Gwyneth paused during the break in the music. She fanned her heated cheeks repeatedly, attempting to cool herself. Lord Henley glanced down at her. His lips were tight, his eyes dark with need. She had seen the same look on the faces of many men, but never on the face of the only man who mattered.

She wanted to see the same burning desire and possessiveness in the eyes of her childhood infatuation as she knew blazed in her eyes when she looked at the impossible but dazzling Viscount Ashworth.

The gentleman, newly arrived, had barely glanced at her despite the new gown made especially to entice the hard-headed rake. Her friend and dress designer, Amelia, obsessed with the simplicity of Greek togas, had crisscrossed sky blue silk across Gwyneth's ample chest with a dramatic décolletage. The back of the gown was draped in the same manner with a revealing V. It was a simple design, but sensual in the way the fabric clung to her body.

She felt alluring and hopeful that tonight Ash would finally throw off all the restraints. She had felt his eyes on her back, knowing he watched her as she gaily danced the intricate pattern she had recently learned from her French dance master.

Lord Henley offered his arm as the quadrille ended. "May I take you to the refreshment table for a glasAs of punch? This new French dance is very demanding."

"Thank you. I'm not thirsty. Can you please take me to my dear friend, Miss Bonnington?"

Lord Henley's eyes clouded with emotion. Gwyneth couldn't refuse the dance, but she needed to escape the gentleman before he embarrassed himself. She wanted to spare him the pain of rejection. After five marriage proposals this season, she had become somewhat of an expert in recognizing the signs of imminent declaration.

Lord Henley escorted Gwyneth to Amelia, who had also finished dancing and now stood alone.

"Thank you, sir, for the dance." Gwyneth did a brief curtsy.

Lord Henley bowed. "It was my pleasure." He hesitated, then sharply nodded his head. She didn't want to be unkind, but there was no reason to pretend interest and encourage hope when there was none.

They watched Lord Henley circle to the other side of the room.

Amelia hid her face behind her fan, her bright eyes dancing in merriment. "Another stricken gentleman."

"I believe he was about to ask if he could call on my brother tomorrow. I think I did an excellent job of extricating myself before Lord Henley declared his feelings."

"Lord Henley is quite a catch. He's heir to a vast fortune. His interest can't be limited only to your dowry."

"Thank you. I'm glad it isn't only money that makes me attractive."

Gwyneth liked to believe it was her wit, her sparkling eyes, but she knew her position as sister to an earl and heiress to a hefty inheritance gave her a definite cache with the gentleman. And it was just like Amelia to tease her.

"Your following of swains has nothing to do with your luscious figure, your dramatic looks, or your amiable personality. My unique skill as a designer has brought all these gentleman to swoon at your feet." Amelia snickered, which made Gwyneth laugh.

Tears were running down Gwyneth's cheeks. "You do know how to level a woman's confidence."

The comment drove both to louder laughter.

Gwyneth noticed that Ash had turned in her direction. He smiled.

Lost in the merriment, she smiled back before she remembered her resolution not to appear as a puppy, waiting at his feet for a pat on the head. She could hide her feelings as well as he did. Forbidden by some unwritten gentleman's code, Ash considered her off limits. She wasn't sure if it was the age difference of eight years, his rakish past, or her position as his best friend's younger sister.

He still kept her at a distance, maintaining that she was a mere youngster and they were simply childhood friends. She had spent the entire season trying to convince him otherwise, but she was tiring of the game.

Amelia hadn't missed the little exchange between her and Ash. Amelia and she had become close since Henrietta, Amelia's best friend, had married Gwyneth's brother. They consoled each other over the loss of the couple who now had interest only in each other.

"There are rumors..."

Gwyneth didn't like the way Amelia's voice grew quiet and serious. Her heart thumped against her chest.

"Rumors?"

"Ash is seeking an alliance with Lady Charolois."

Gwyneth tried to swallow away the pain that lodged in her throat. "Who is Lady Charolois?"

Amelia put her hand on Gwyneth's arm. The gesture of friendship only heightened the sinking feeling.

"She is a widow. Gossip is that her husband was a French marquis who was guillotined. She recently arrived in London. I believe she is a relative of Sir Cornwell."

"Is she here now?"

"Yes, she is in conversation with Lord Ramsay."

A tingle of awareness lifted the fine hairs on Gwyneth's neck. Amelia wasn't privy to the fact that Sir Ramsay had been Head of British Intelligence. Lady Charolois might be part of the network of spies that worked for her brother who had assumed Sir Ramsay's position.

Hope fluttered in her breast. Ash's interest in Lady Charolois might not indicate a return to his rakish past, but a mission. She had deduced that Ash's years away in France had been in service to the crown, not for wild dissipation as he allowed everyone to believe.

Lord Ramsay shifted his position. Gwyneth glimpsed a small, blond, well-endowed, woman. Her stomach churned at the lady's radiant beauty.

"She looks British."

Gwyneth and Amelia turned their heads to see Ash, resplendent in a black coat, his broad shoulders hugging his jacket, making his way toward Lady Charolois.

Amelia's sympathetic look made it all worse. "I don't want you to make the mistake, I did. Don't waste the best years of your life waiting and dreaming of something that may never come to pass." Amelia and she had become closer when they both realized they shared the same affliction— unrequited love. Amelia had never spoken this frankly or despondently. Her friend had been waiting for Henrietta's brother, Michael, for years.

She turned and looked at Amelia whose face was tight with stifled emotions. "I'm so sorry. I didn't realize how badly you felt."

"I don't think I knew what I was missing until I saw how happy Henrietta has become."

"Yes, it's the same with my brother. They're disgustingly happy."

Amelia snorted. "Look, the happy couple just arrived."

Cord and Henrietta stood at the door of the ballroom. It was obvious that neither were aware of the intimate bond that enveloped them. Cord held Henrietta close to his body. His harsh countenance softened as he gazed down on her. Even from thirty feet away, she could see Henrietta's face turn a deep blush.

"As I said, disgustingly happy," Gwyneth scoffed. "I've decided to go to the Edworth's Christmas house party and you need to come with me. We need to get away from London, away from..."

Gwyneth didn't want to admit that she was already dreading the holidays with the happy couple. Not that she didn't adore her brother and his simply wonderful wife, but she was ready to have someone special to share her favorite holiday.

"My brothers will be there. You haven't met my oldest brother. He has a way with the ladies, but he is a true gentleman. And rumor has it that Prinny might make an appearance," Amelia said.

"Really? The Prince Regent is going to spend Christmas away from his father?"

"As you know, there is no deep affection between them. The king doesn't approve of his son's lavish living."

"But still it's Christmas, a time for families to be together." As she spoke, she realized that her family had changed—no longer just herself, Cord and Aunt Euphemia.

She had always loved the holiday and romanticized the season as a time of magic and hope. Because of the loss of her oldest brother to a tragic riding accident, her parents made a big effort to create a special holiday for her, but there was always a pall of sadness in the household. Though she had wonderful memories because Cord always came home to share them with her.

She had hoped to spend the holiday in Ash's arms, planning their future. Talk about fantasies. It was time to take decisive steps toward her own future and stop waiting on the dashing gentleman who had been a

young girl's fantasy. It was time to
take control of her life.

Ignoring the logical conclusions of
her brain, she again led with her
heart's true desire. "Let's join Sir
Ramsay. I haven't seen him in an
age."

"You want to join Ash and Lady
Charolois?" Amelia's voice sounded a
bit strangled.

"No, I want to visit with Sir
Ramsay. He's a longtime family
friend. I'm happy to greet this new
lady and offer my friendship. I think
that she might be in need of friends."
Gwyneth marched toward the group.
She knew her shoulders were pulled
back, her chin thrust forward. She had
the look of determination that told
those who knew her best to tread
cautiously.

"You aren't going to do anything
rash? Cause a scene?" Amelia
whispered behind her fan.

"Me? Cause a scene? I'm too mature
of a woman for such childish displays."
She needed to see Ash's reaction to the
lady before she relinquished her
illusions about him—before she

decided whether to attend a Christmas party far away from him.

Ash had purposefully positioned himself with his back to her so she couldn't see him work his appealing charm and flash his crooked, mischievous smile at the lady. Sir Ramsay was the first to see the ladies approaching. His taut, weathered face softened into a warm greeting.

"How lovely to greet my favorite neighbor. Lady Gwyneth and Miss Amelia. Well met."

Ash turned around sharply when he heard her name. His eyes flared and then his lips pulled back in an outraged glower as he looked down at Amelia's creation and her barely covered décolletage. His reaction made her heart palpitate. She felt his whole body tighten next to her, heard the barely audible hitch in his breath.

A warm feeling spread through Gwyneth as she observed Ash's restrained reaction to her new gown. He wasn't interested in Lady Charolois.

His only response to her was a curt nod of his head. "Lady Gwyneth and Miss Amelia."

Sir Ramsay turned toward her and Amelia and asked, "Have you had the pleasure of meeting Lady Charolois?"

"We haven't had the... pleasure..." Gwyneth stared at Ash, her chin raised in defiance of making the lady's acquaintance.

Ash's eyes narrowed with suspicion.

She had trouble not smiling at him. Oh, he wasn't interested in the other lady.

All three ladies curtsied. The blond beauty was like one of the woodland sprites. She had an ethereal quality that might fool many men, but Gwyneth hadn't missed the lady's calculating glance as she and Amelia approached.

Sir Ramsay broke the strained silence. "We were just discussing our plans for the Christmas season."

"Are you staying in town for the holidays, Lady Charolois?" Gwyneth asked.

Ash cleared his throat.

The lady's nervous flicker of her round blue eyes might have hoodwinked Britain's top agents, but Gwyneth recognized when a woman had plans. And like the calculating lady, Gwyneth had her own schemes.

"I'm attending Lord Edworth's country party. I've no family and find London's smog so weary for the holidays." Her French accent lilted her husky voice, making her sound exotic and enticing to the male population.

"That is an amazing coincidence. Amelia and I were just discussing our plans to attend the same party."

"What?" Ash asked in a rude manner "Cord is allowing you to spend the holidays away from your family?"

"I haven't discussed my holiday plans with Cord. Amelia and I've decided we needed to break away from our familiar childhood merriments, to forge new ways of celebrating. Isn't that so, Amelia?" Gwyneth enjoyed watching Ash's grey eyes darken and the pulsing beat in his jaw thicken.

Amelia had been watching the by-plays, eyes wide with surprise. She fluttered her fan in front of her face.

"Also, we've decided like you, Lady Charolois that the season grows tiresome and we need a change in scene." Gwyneth waved with her hands toward the dance floor. "I mean in the weather."

Gwyneth could feel Ash's body thrumming next to hers, his heat wrapping around her. She was having a grand time baiting the gentleman. He thought he could ignore her. Fiddlesticks to that. And now, it was time to do a bit of her own spying. "We've heard that the Prince Regent will be attending. Will you be retiring to your estate, Sir Ramsay, or will you venture to Bath and the house party?"

Sir Ramsay harrumphed and cleared his throat. "I won't be, but Ash is considering attending." Poor Ramsay, as his aunt affectionately called him, looked confounded. Nothing like shaking up Britain's top intelligence agent.

Ash's face registered no outward reaction. The man was definitely a very skilled spy since anyone not thoroughly acquainted with him would be unable to glean that Viscount Ashworth was livid, stroking mad. The little tic above his right eye pulsed and his usual cool grey eyes smoldered with hidden emotions.

The petite French lady clapped her hands in feigned delight or maybe not feigned since who could resist Ash, the blond Adonis? His golden curls framed his chiseled countenance and bright eyes. Unlike other gentleman, he didn't seem to care greatly about his appearance. His hair was brushed back from his face in a haphazard way, as if he had just risen from bed and run his fingers through his hair.

The thought of Ash and a bed sent a wave of pleasurable sensations through her body.

Ash watched Gwyneth with a speculative regard. He missed nothing. Her dark eyes widened and her lips parted as if in excitement. His entire body tightened in response. He wanted to kiss those lips. Oh, the things he wanted to do to her and those luscious lips.

"Lord Ashworth?"

He realized everyone was waiting for his response. "I haven't made any plans yet, but with all these lovely ladies attending, this party must not to be missed." Ash's voice had taken on a seductive tenor.

"Oh, nicely said, Lord Ashworth," the little lady chirped.

He bowed his head to the lady. "Lady Charolois, is your dance card full or may I have the pleas...the honor of one of tonight's dances?"

Gwyneth had to bite on the side of her mouth to keep from laughing out loud when she caught Ash's eye as he was about to say the word "pleasure" and changed to "honor."

"That would be delightful, my lord." The lady's voice was breathless and seductive.

Gwyneth wanted to say aloud, "Men really don't fall for winded coyness, do they?"

Lady Charolois' calculated smile and charms seemed to be working. Ash's steely grey eyes had warmed and he had the gall to bestow upon the lady the smile Gwyneth believed should only be reserved for her—the one that made him look young and carefree, like the youth she had fallen in love with at the ripe age of ten years.

"If you'll excuse us. I've promised this dance to Lady Gwyneth." Ash gripped her arm tightly as he led her toward the dance floor.

"You didn't give me time to say good night to your newest paramour. Really, Ash, she looks a bit old for you."

Ash stopped at the edge of the dance floor and looked into Gwyneth's unfathomable eyes. She had the same mischievous look she had in childhood, when she would follow Cord and him and think she had bested them in some prank. But this wasn't some childish game. This was dangerous.

"You have no idea what you're meddling in. Walk with me. I need to speak with you."

She bit down on her lower lip, bringing attention to the warm, moist, pink surface. Hot desire flared through his body again at the irresistible temptation she presented. He couldn't get sidetracked when he had a mission, a serious mission. The minx wet her plump lower lip with her tongue. Was she doing this to addle him?

"I'm not meddling. I wanted to meet the lady who has attracted your notice. We're old family friends. I don't think the lady could misconstrue my interest."

"Gwyneth." He tried to sound authoritative, but instead his voice came out plaintive.

He led her out the doors to a darkened corner on the balcony. He needed to stop her interference in his mission while not drawing attention to their relationship. He didn't want his enemies to know of his regard for her.

He couldn't let her get close to these people. He hated what he needed to do, but it was for her safety. He couldn't let her be involved. Once he had broken the ring of spies, he'd make it up to her. She understood how he felt about her. Keenly observant, Gwyneth knew him better than anyone.

She stepped closer to him, her enticing body wrapped as a present in soft, seductive blue silk, ready for him to open. His breathing deepened to aggressive surges. He didn't dare look down at her creamy white breasts or he might not be responsible for what happened next.

"Ash?" The way she said his name in a throaty, seductive voice sent a bolt of desire straight up his spine. Her black, slanted eyes were wide and mysterious, staring into his. She had no idea how potent an effect that look precipitated. Or maybe she did.

He was so damn tired of this spy business, always postponing his needs for country. If he gave her any hint of his purpose in attending the country party, she'd be dogging his footsteps, trying to prove she could help him. He didn't want her as a spy. He knew the toll the subterfuge and lies took on a person.

"You must celebrate Christmas with Cord and your aunt. The country party is not for the likes of you. The society who attend Prinny's parties are..."

"Then you're not going?" She scrutinized him with those innocent eyes.

"I'm going, but you're not. The party is for older, experienced women, which you are not."

"But that is exactly why I've decided to go. I might not be able to advance my age, but I can acquire experience." She leaned closer and whispered tauntingly, "I'm so weary of being kissed by honorable gentlemen."

Every muscle in his body constricted in reaction. "Who has been kissing you?" He actually growled the words then grabbed her shoulders. "And do not tell me that Henley is involved. He's a rake of the first order."

She batted her long, dark lashes at him. "Takes one to know one."

She was soft, warm and pliant. He wanted to run his hands along her silky skin.

"He's pledged that he's done with his wildness. He said he'd give up all women if I'd consent..."

Ash couldn't suppress the surge of pure masculine possessiveness and anger. Henley wouldn't be pursuing Cord's innocent sister unless he was seriously interested. He pulled her closer, his hands tightening on her shoulders. "You let him kiss you?"

A tiny crack had begun to erode his confidence. He assumed that Gwyneth would be his when he could finally break away from the damn spy business.

When she tried to pull away, he wrapped his arms around her, inhaling deeply her womanly scent of wildflowers, outdoors and the special scent of Gwyneth. He wanted her against him, to feel her woman's softness melting around him.

"I would never kiss and tell—that would be unladylike. I've had five marriage proposals this season. You can't expect a girl not to explore whether she wants the gentleman."

There it was again—that innocent look. How she played him, like the violinist playing a sonata in the ballroom.

"I won't be distracted by the change in topics. We were discussing why you must not attend the Christmas party." As always in interacting with her, he felt light and young. She made him smile, the minx.

"Are you distracted by me?" She fingered the lapel of his jacket. For a country miss, she was an exotic temptress, more so than any highly paid courtesan.

He stopped her hand from wandering by closing his hand over hers. "Gwyneth, I forbid you to go to the party."

She pulled her hand away. "I don't need your permission to go to the party."

"Then I'm going to speak to Cord about your plans."

"You've no right to interfere with my holiday plans." A tendril of her thick black hair hung across her right eye. With her strong chin and delectable chest thrust forward, she looked like a pagan queen ready for battle.

"I've every right, and you know it." He pulled her hard against him and took her lips in a deliberate, demanding way. He held her tightly as his tongue darted in and out of her warm moisture. Once he felt her soften against him, he lightened the pressure of his lips and ran his tongue along the edge of her lower lip. "So sweet." And so innocent. What was he doing kissing her on the balcony. He had to get back to the ballroom and he didn't want to think about her reaction to his public pursuit of Lady Charolois.

She ran her hand through his hair, down his neck. "Oh, Ash." She crushed her voluptuous curves closer. "Our first real kiss." Her voice was filled with wonder.

Perhaps he had made their first kiss too carnal, but she had pushed him. She was always pushing him, but clearly they both liked the tantalizing result.

"I must get you back to your aunt. She'll have my hide if she knew we were out on the balcony."

"Aunt Euphemia is playing cards. She won't mind."

"Oh, I think she'll mind a great deal if I ruin your reputation. And Cord..."

"I wouldn't mind..." There was the young girl he knew—always testing the limits. And she was a challenging provocation—the way she posed with dewy lips, the moonlight dancing across her creamy, desirable décolletage.

He placed her hand on his arm. He avoided looking at her since, if he did, he'd need to kiss her again, and then they would never stop. He needed to get back to his goal in attending this ball. He was glad he and Gwyneth had come to an amiable agreement. He'd always enjoy the way they settled their differences.

CHAPTER TWO

Gwyneth leaned back against the velvet cushions of the carriage and looked at her energetic aunt. Aunt Euphemia never divulged her age, but Gwyneth knew she had passed sixty years. Following another demanding late night, her aunt didn't look the least bit tired even though it was nearly dawn.

"Well, spit it out. I can tell you're in a taking."

"I'm not. Well, maybe a little... Aunt Euphemia, how do I become a spy?"

Her aunt slapped her purple draped knee and guffawed. "Not the question I was expecting." Her favorite aunt tilted her head to one side, causing her turban filled with flowers to lean precariously.

"Gel, what's going through that spinning brain of yours?"

"I want to help our country. I've talents, but don't know how to use them. I want to be like you and Henrietta."

"What has brought this on? Something with Ash?"

"Yes... no... I don't know."

"Didn't Amelia's newest creation get the results you expected from Ash?"

"He kissed me."

Her aunt chortled. "Well, it's about time."

"He was worried that you'd be upset."

"Was he now? It makes me happy to hear he's still intimated by the likes of an old woman. Well, if he's declared his intentions, why are you thinking about becoming a spy?"

"I do love him and want to be his wife, but I want what Henrietta and Cord have. Cord respects her for her talents, not just because she's beautiful and wonderful. I want Ash to respect me. Right now, he thinks of me as a silly young girl, always following after him."

Aunt Euphemia smiled. "Yes, I didn't think you'd ever settle for less. But men don't think that way. They feel their job is to protect women and keep them safe, away from the workings of the world."

"Pshaw. With you and Henrietta as an example, how can Ash think I'd be satisfied not being part of his entire life? I want to be his partner."

"What are you planning? He won't take lightly to your interference."

"When I told Ash that I planned to spend Christmas at Edworth's, he forbade me from attending. When I told him he didn't have the right, he said he would speak to Cord. Aunt Euphemia, can't you go with me to the Edworth's party?"

"I don't enjoy travel in the winter." Her aunt rubbed her knees. "My old bones. And I planned to stay with Cord and Henrietta, Charles and Edward. Is this the party that the Prince Regent is supposed to attend?"

"Yes. I don't know what all the fuss is about, but Ash is working on something with Sir Ramsay and Lady Charolois, and he's forbidden me to participate."

"Interesting."

"Ash is getting very friendly with Lady Charolois. At first I thought she might work for the Intelligence Office, but the way she was looking at Ash, I don't believe she's in our country's employ. Ash is trying to court her favor. I could be of help, make friends with the lady. I'm very observant."

Aunt Euphemia was shaking her head. "You are very perceptive, but if they're worried that Lady Charolois has surreptitious connections, I don't think putting yourself in that position would be wise. If she is a spy, she might use your connection to Cord against you."

"I wouldn't be doing anything to alert the lady. And you must agree that ladies spend a great deal of time together at house parties, and I might glean information that Ash could never obtain."

"Let me talk to Ramsay and find out what the concerns are. Then we can decide."

"I knew I could count on you, Aunt Euphemia. You're a dear."

"Don't lay it on too thick. I didn't say we'd attend."

"Oh, I can always tell when you're interested."

CHAPTER THREE

Ash paced in front of Cord's massive desk. What could possibly be delaying his ever-punctual friend? Cord was usually at his office by nine am, sharp to deal with his heavy responsibilities as the Head of British Secret Intelligence.

Ten minutes later, Cord sauntered into the office. His posture relaxed—lacking his usual determined demeanor.

"Ash, what brings you to the office so early? Have you news about the threat?"

Cord handed his personal secretary his wet coat and umbrella. Cord hummed as he walked to the window where the rain beat against the windows. "Wonderful morning, isn't it?"

What the hell? His friend never hummed and it was a God-awful day with torrential rain and wind. "I've never seen you act like this."

Cord turned back from the window with a wide grin across his face. "Acting how?"

"Cheerful."

Cord gave a hearty belly laugh. "You make it sound sinful to be happy."

Ash wasn't happy, and his closest friend's obvious pleasure only worsened his mood.

Since Cord had married Henrietta, his entire manner had transformed. His childhood friend had returned to the happy young man he had been before his older brother had died in a tragic riding accident. Cord now laughed readily and was openly affectionate with his friends and family. The change had been more than extraordinary, as was evident in his cheery mood this morning.

"I received wonderful...rather miraculous news this morning."

"Wonderful" and "miraculous" would never have crossed the lips of the old, cynical Cord. Ash didn't want his friend to be unhappy, but this dramatic change was hard to stomach.

Ash moved toward the window in the gloomy, dim office to catch a closer look at his friend's face. How could his friend look so completely different? The usual tired, world-weary lines around Cord's eyes and mouth had vanished. The man looked blissful, at peace.

"This miracle is more than you walking around with an idiotic grin on your face?"

"I'm to be a father."

The news hit like a blow to Ash's chest. "A father? This is a shock." His entire familiar world shifted below his feet.

"Who'd believe that in a few short months, I'd be a married man and now an expectant father." Cord shook his head.

"Congratulations, old man." Ash clasped his arm around his friend's shoulder. "We need to toast the auspicious announcement."

"Yes, a drink seems in order. I haven't had time to grasp the news. Rather a surprising way to start the morning."

Cord walked to the heavy mahogany cabinet and opened the door to reach his most prized carafe of port. He poured each of them a snifter of ruby red liquid. Both men inhaled the heavy fruity scent.

Ash raised his glass. "To Lady Henrietta."

"To my amazing wife." Cord's lips curved into a satisfied smile and a look of wistfulness filled his eyes.

Ash's own emotions were in turmoil. He felt the distance growing wider between himself and his closest childhood friend. He didn't know what it felt like to make the ultimate of commitment to a woman. His thoughts immediately went to Gwyneth as a mother. She'd be incredible—gentle and nurturing.

"You mustn't share the news. We just found out this morning, and Henrietta wants to tell my aunt and sister when we are all together."

"Speaking of your sister, how could you allow her to go to the Edworth's Christmas party?" Ash couldn't keep the hostility out of his voice. "What the hell were you thinking?"

Cord laughed loudly and slapped Ash on the back. "Allow? You've got a lot to learn about women. You never tell women that you're *allowing them* to do anything. That gets their backs up and then you can never, never win. Trust me—as an old married man."

Ash wasn't sure he liked this new side of Cord. He was a male and should support the male point of view. "You've only been married six weeks."

"And speaking of my sister, you'd better not be applying your experience before the wedding."

Immediately Ash felt his face turning red. Hell, he never blushed. It was feminine.

Snifter in hand, Cord sat at his desk as Ash sat across from him in one of the hefty chairs. Whenever Ash flashed to his demanding kiss and the way Gwyneth melted for him, a surge of hunger hurtled through him.

Cord suddenly didn't look as congenial as his eyes narrowed on Ash's face. Ash took the offensive. "Why would you put Gwyneth's safety at risk? You know what is at stake."

"You made the party much more alluring to Gwyneth by forbidding her to go and by telling her that you'd talk with me."

"She told you?"

"No, she told Aunt Euphemia who told me. I'm trying to help you. Benefit from my mistakes with Henrietta. I forbade her to be involved with the danger surrounding her brother's disappearance. Her response was to immediately circumvent me and almost get herself killed."

"I don't know what to expect at the party, but my intelligence is solid. There is going to be a threat against Prinny, possibly from the French Jacobins. It might be nothing, or it could be deadly."

"But why would the French extremists want to threaten the Prince Regent? We share common goals. We want to get rid of Napoleon as badly they do. The Jacobins hate Napoleon for making himself Emperor and abandoning all of his liberal leanings. He got rid of all of his Jacobin supporters by either murdering or exiling them. Why come after the English?"

"It makes no sense. But I need to assume it's a threat against Prinny, who had made it public that he plans to attend," Ash said.

"I agree that we have to take the threat seriously, but I hate when I can't deduce the logic. Prinny isn't political at all. He's much more interested in his art collection and dissipation."

"Yes, but he is the Prince Regent. And his father is severely ill."

"I understand, but the threat against Prinny should be by Napoleon supporters, not Jacobins."

"You will warn him?"

"I've an audience with him this afternoon to tell him of the possible threat and to suggest he remain in London for the holiday."

"I'd rest easier if he didn't come."

"Prinny is like Gwyneth. If you warn him against attending, he'll want to come simply to make a point."

"God, this is a mess. I don't want her to attend when we don't know what we're up against."

"She can be a help to you. Gwyneth is quite observant and very skilled with people."

"You want me to confide in your sister about our work with the French spy underground and their possible intelligence that there might a threat against the Prince Regent at this party?"

"God, no. I didn't mean that you should tell her about the danger, but if you tell her you're following a lead tying Lady Charolois to French spies, she'll feel more involved. And she might be able to observe things that you can't. Women are much more sensitive to the nuances of society."

"Your sister is a sheltered, innocent woman. She knows nothing about French spies. She will be an added distraction. I'll be worrying about her safety instead of focusing on the danger to the prince."

Cord raised his eyebrows. "Gwyneth might surprise you."

"Why have you had a change of heart? The Cord I knew would never countenance his sister involved in spy business."

"Marriage to Henrietta. I'd never considered how resourceful ladies can be. And Aunt Euphemia feels you're doing Gwyneth a great injustice by not allowing her to be involved on the periphery of your work."

"Your aunt, the foremost spy in our business, thinks Gwyneth should be involved in a clandestine operation?"

"My aunt, like me, thinks it will be a mistake to have Gwyneth working on her own, trying to prove to you that she can be helpful. My aunt believes if you're there to guide Gwyneth, she won't rush into danger. It's safer to make her an ally and work with her, instead of leaving her to go off alone."

He shook his head in disbelief. "This is a half-cocked plan. It could become perilous."

"With any other man, I wouldn't consider placing my sister in the situation. But my aunt and I both agree that you are totally capable of keeping her safe."

Ash stood up and paced. The walls felt as if they were suffocating him, closing in on him. "I refuse to have Gwyneth at the party. I can't imagine the scenario."

"Well, I have it on the best authority, that of my wife and my aunt, that unless you include Gwyneth in your work, you'll lose her."

Ash turned sharply. He couldn't control the savage desperation in his voice. "What the hell does that mean?" He wanted to wipe the knowing smirk off Cord's face.

"My sister has had five marriage proposals. Lord Henley is very interested in her, and according to Henrietta, Gwyneth likes him greatly. Right now the way I see it, you have the advantage of her girlhood infatuation. The ladies are of the opinion that you need to start to see her as a competent woman or she might look to a man who doesn't remember her in short skirts and curls. Women like men to see them as capable—or that's what I've learned from my wife."

"Capable of handling spies?

"My wife did."

"Your wife is an exception."

"I agree." There was that lost sappy look on Cord's face again.

"But Gwyneth is so young."

"Yes, and smart, brave and ready to help her country. After the king's demonstration at Hyde Park of our military strength against the possible invasion of Napoleon, she wants to be of service. I'm proud of her."

"But our job is to protect the women, not have them involved in war."

Cord laughed again. He might have to throttle his friend, new baby or not.

"All you have to do is ask Gwyneth to let you know if anyone or anything seems out of place at the party. You don't have to go into any lengthy explanations."

"Does your aunt plan to chaperone Gwyneth for the party? I'd feel better if the old girl was keeping an eye on the situation."

"My aunt has reassured me that she will come to the party. She is tracking down an old contact who might have more information about the Jacobins. Gwyneth and Amelia have already departed. Aunt Euphemia is hoping to leave in two days' time. Are you leaving today?"

"I went to Edworth a few days ago to get everything in place. I've got Brinsley in the stables and men in the house."

"Keep me posted. And send a man if you discover any information on the threat. If it comes to it, I'll go to the king to stop the Prince Regent from attending."

CHAPTER FOUR

Gwyneth peered upward at the impressive façade of Edworth mansion. The stone manor house looked like a castle with turrets dwarfing each corner and an enormous entranceway from medieval times.

She envisioned the large wooden door decorated with holly and ivy soon to come. Here was the perfect setting for a Christmas party.

A footman held an umbrella over her head as she looked at the edifice. Amelia had rushed out of the rain to the entrance and the waiting butler. Her friend had wanted to freshen up before meeting the other guests.

The sheets of rain and gray clouds couldn't dampen her cheery mood.

Gwyneth hoped for snow to blanket the muddy hills behind her. Christmas was a season of hope and goodwill, and she felt exhilaration for the adventure she was about to embark on with Ash.

Before leaving London, Aunt Euphemia had confided in Gwyneth that Ash had agreed to her assistance in his clandestine work, including attending the house party. She couldn't believe the craftiness of her aunt and Henrietta—implying to Cord and Ash that she was interested in Lord Henley. She still had a lot to learn from her aunt and sister-in-law on spy-craft and dealing with the male species.

A towering, authoritative butler waited for Gwyneth. She hurried up the stone steps into the foyer.

"Lady Gwyneth, welcome to Edworth House. I'm Brunton." He had an accent that she initially might have thought was French, but quickly realized must be Welsh. That would explain the singsong rhythm of his speech.

"It's lovely to have finally arrived. I've never visited Edworth house, but

my parents were frequent visitors and
spoke often of the friendliness of those
who live and work here and the
efficiency of a well-run house."
Gwyneth looked into the butler's eyes
waiting for a softening in his formal,
stiff manner.

"Milady, I'm newly in service at
Edworth house." His small eyes flitted
away from her close inspection.

She couldn't hide her
disappointment that Brunton didn't
know her parents. She hadn't confided
in anyone that coming to the estate of
her father's close friend for Christmas
was a way to feel closer to her parents.
It also suited her purpose with Ash
perfectly.

"Well, Brunton. You and I are both
new to Edworth house, but that won't
deter our holiday celebration." She
stripped off her sodden pelisse.

"Yes, milady." Brunton didn't meet
her eyes and obviously didn't share
her enthusiasm. Cord always warned
her that she was too familiar with the
staff. Growing up in the country, she
was used to more relaxed manners.
Obviously Brunton was from Lord

Edworth's London home and embraced the proper ways of society.

"There are refreshments in the drawing room unless you'd like to retire to your room."

"Thank you, Brunton. I'll join everyone in the drawing room. I'm very excited to meet the other guests." She was starving and didn't want to take the time to freshen herself as Amelia had.

Gwyneth couldn't contain her eagerness for her first house party and a Christmas party. A haughty, bald butler couldn't dampen her excitement.

A footman walked ahead, leading her toward the library.

As the door was opened, Gwyneth saw Ash standing close to Lady Charolois. He leaned toward her in an intimate way, his shoulders and head bent to her as if she were the sun and he a flower.

Fiery jealousy sent flames flicking down her spine. Were Ash and the lady involved? She couldn't bear the thought. Her brother had reassured her before she left for the party that Ash's intentions were honorable, but years of watching women pursue Ash and him allowing himself to be caught burned through her body like acid.

Her eagerness and enthusiasm for Christmas and the party plummeted.

How had Ash arrived at the party before her and Amelia? Had he travelled with Lady Charolois? Jealousy was a horrible sensation. Gnawing at one's well-being.

She stood paralyzed at the door until she heard her name.

Lord Henley walked toward her. She tried to mask her surprise. She hadn't expected the gentleman would be attending. This was going to get complicated. She didn't want Ash to know of Aunt Euphemia's and Henrietta's subterfuge and that her interest in Lord Henley was a ruse.

His genuine smile of regard helped to diminish her worries. "Lady Gwyneth. I've been awaiting your arrival. How was your journey? I hope you're not too fatigued by the dreadful weather?"

"Lord Henley, I didn't know you were attending the house party. I thought you'd be returning to your estate."

Lord Henley raised her hand to his lips, holding her gaze. "I changed my plans when I heard that you were attending."

Oh, not good. The sinking feeling in her stomach returned, and her hunger disappeared. Now what should she say? She genuinely liked the gentleman.

"This is my first house party and it's the Christmas Season. Could anything be more wonderful?"

Lord Henley's eyes darkened and his voice got gravelly. "Most assuredly." His eyes bored into hers.

She felt like a terrible charlatan, but she didn't want to hurt his feelings.

"Am I interrupting anything?" Ash came from behind her. His deep baritone voice had the effect of a feather trailing down her spine, but she could also hear his antagonism.

"Ashworth, I didn't expect to see you here," Lord Henley said.

"Lady Gwyneth." Ash tilted his head in a slight bow. "Henley, I'm also surprised to find you here. What brings you to Bath?"

Oh, my goodness. A faint color tinged his cheekbones as the worldly gentleman, Lord Henley, stuttered, "I've just...arrived."

Recognizing the poor man's embarrassment, Gwyneth could feel her own cheeks color. "Was your travel difficult, Lord Henley?"

"The trip was easy. And what about your trip, Ashworth?"

"I am newly arrived, but I'm only here for a few days before I travel home to celebrate with my family," Ash said.

Her attention toward Ash intensified. Did he really plan to leave before Christmas or was this part of an elaborate subterfuge?

She had to speak to Ash alone to find out who he was really here to spy on.

"Lady Gwyneth, may I get you some refreshment after your long journey?" Lord Henley asked.

She smiled warmly at Lord Henley. "Thank you. I would enjoy a little something to eat." Who was she kidding, she was ready to eat an entire meal.

"Shall I prepare you a plate?"

She nodded in acquiescence. He was a most kind gentleman. She must find him another woman to capture his interest. She considered the debutantes of the season who might be a good match for the very handsome earl.

"I can't believe I'm witnessing Henley acting like a besotted fool," Ash muttered under his breath.

"What?"

"With you working your charms on him, he doesn't have a chance. I saw the way you got all moon-eyed with him before I came over. The man needs to grow some ballocks."

"Of all the crude comments. For your information, I wasn't making any moon-eyes at him. I was being friendly."

"Friendly? Henley wants more than friendly."

Ash's face was contorted with emotions she didn't recognize. "What is it Ash? I've never seen that look before."

His voice was rough. "Never mind. We need to talk about this little enterprise you've embarked upon."

"Yes, I'm so excited to have you tell me my assignment, what you need me to do."

"You don't need to..." He rubbed the blond stubble growing on his strong, square chin. It made her all warm and wobbly inside to see his manly features.

"When everyone is getting ready for dinner, meet me in the conservatory. It is in the east wing of the house."

"Of course. I'll dress for dinner before meeting you," she gushed with enthusiasm. The adventure with Ash was finally beginning.

"Say nothing of the meeting to anyone including Amelia. Do you understand?" His voice had the same patronizing tone she remembered from childhood.

"Yes, I understand. And I can be discrete."

Ash rolled his eyes toward the sky. "You and the word 'discrete' can't be said in the same sentence."

And with that *bon mot,* he walked away.

CHAPTER FIVE

Gwyneth had dressed carefully for the secret rendezvous. Her heart beat a rapid tattoo against her chest as she peered furtively out her bedroom door. Waiting for her maid to leave had been unbearable. Lizzie had wanted to fuss with Gwyneth's simple chignon. She had finally submitted to a more complicated style with braids at her temple and an emerald necklace and drop earrings. It had been easier to give in to Lizzie's ministrations than to explain why she'd dressed early.

Gwyneth lifted the hem of her emerald silk dress. She had chosen the color for the holiday season, but she wore it tonight as a camouflage to blend in with the greenery.

Amelia didn't know that the simple elegance of her design was perfect for moving stealthily. Gwyneth smoothed her hand along the lustrous fabric that hugged her waist and fell in rich folds to her feet. Although cut low and resting on her shoulders, the dress was perfect for the easy movement of a spy. She had worn her soft slippers to minimize the noise as she descended the stairs.

She had wanted to add a sprig of holly to the ribbon that wrapped around her waist. But Lady Edworth had delayed the gathering of the holiday greens until the blasted rain stopped.

Anticipation and apprehension thrummed along her nerves as she slowly made her way down the long, narrow hallway. She could hear bits of conversations behind the closed doors, but the hallway remained empty.

She descended the long marble staircase. Brunton directed the footmen from the center of the foyer as they scurried between the salon and the dining room.

Surprise registered across Brunton's face when he saw her, but he quickly hid any reaction and returned to his usual stony countenance. "Lady Gwyneth, may I be of service?"

She knew he wanted to ask why she had arrived early for dinner, but no butler worth his salt would question the thinking or behavior of a lady or a gentleman.

"Brunton, can you direct me to the conservatory? I'm very interested in the study of botany and couldn't wait to see Lady Edworth's collection. My mother often spoke of the amazing, rare species." She was confident that the Edworth's conservatory, like the whole estate, would be exemplary and Brunton would have no reason not to believe her. That her mother had never shown interest in plants and that Gwyneth was the only Rathbourne fascinated by botany was known to no one but her family.

She gave her sweetest, most charming smile—the one that always melted the most hardened, including her brother and aunt. The dour man wasn't as easily swayed.

"I'm not familiar with Lady Edworth's plant collection, but I'm happy to have Thomas escort you."

"Thank you, Brunton. I don't need an escort since I know you're all very busy with the dinner preparations."

Brunton stiffened. His neck and shoulders grew more rigid, which was hard to imagine since the man looked as unbending as a tree trunk.

Brunton opened a door off of the entranceway. "Follow this corridor. The conservatory is at the end, on the east side of the manor. Are you sure, my lady, that you don't want Thomas to accompany you?"

She could barely contain her enthusiasm for her secret appointment with Ash. So far this spy business was invigorating and she could appreciate why her brother and Ash did undercover work. "Thank you, Brunton. I'm sure I can find my way."

She passed the ballroom, now empty, but soon to be filled with happy couples celebrating the most magical time of year. In anticipation of the coming holiday season, she hummed the "Twelve Days of Christmas" as she moved quietly down the corridor.

The conservatory was straight ahead. The door to the expansive glass room was closed. Suddenly the light hairs on her neck and arms stood on end. She turned around quickly, feeling as if someone were watching her. She saw and heard nothing.

Assuming her vivid imagination was getting the better of her, she slowly pulled the door open with a loud squeak. Her heart hammered against her tightened corset, making it hard to breathe. She scanned the dark room searching for Ash. She hadn't thought to bring a candle. She would remember in her next assignment to come prepared.

The humid, warm air enveloped her. Memories of playing alone on cold, wet days in Rathbourne's conservatory rushed through her. Her interest in plants dated back to her lonely childhood days spent among tropical plants, dreaming of exciting exploits.

She could barely see the main path down the center of the conservatory. Her gown dragged on the flagstone, making a swishing sound that resonated loudly. She walked further into the room. In the stillness, all of her senses heightened. Someone else was here. If it were Ash, why didn't he declare himself?

She lifted her gown with both hands, rushing to hide behind a potted Arecaceae, a palm tree from the Americas.

She froze, determined to remain still. She held her breath, afraid that the gush of air she held tightly in her chest might burst out.

Above the clamor of her heart reverberating in her ears, she could hear the distinctive sound of someone in a gown moving on the opposite side of the room. Had she interrupted a tryst?

Unfazed by the presence of a woman, she leaned around the plant to search. Nothing. She heard and saw no one. She leaned a little farther around the giant palm when suddenly she felt a push from behind. Her head jerked as her body was thrust forward. She fell to her hands and knees.

Stunned but not injured, she couldn't get her bearings. She twisted from her position on the ground when she heard the conservatory door opening. A blond woman in a blue gown ran through the door. Lady Charolois, if Gwyneth wasn't mistaken. But the lady couldn't have shoved her.

Anger and fear slammed into her body, making her shaky. Was her assailant still in the conservatory? She slowly and silently pushed herself to a standing position. She needed to get away.

Looking carefully around the darkened room, listening for every sound, chills of cold and hot chased over every inch of her skin.

The door to the conservatory opened, pouring light into the room. She jumped behind the Arecaceae. Her heart accelerated wildly. She waited, her ears drumming with the silence.

"Gwyneth?"

Ash's whispered voice was a balm to her shattered nerves.

She stepped out from the plant. "Ash, I'm here."

He walked toward her. His strong profile and confident walk made her want to run into his arms, but she controlled the impulse.

"Why are you hiding?" He asked in a teasing tone.

"Why were you late?" She didn't like the idea that he'd found her frightened at their first secret rendezvous.

"Late?" He placed one hand on his hip, his tone sardonic. "I didn't realize I was late."

"Never mind. I'm unsettled after my fall."

He inspected her carefully, his light eyes moving over her body. "Did you trip?"

She wasn't quick to get mad, but she felt the anger slowly moving up her spine. Cord and Ash had tormented her relentlessly about her clumsiness when she was a young girl. "First of all, I didn't trip as you suspect. And I wasn't clumsy as a girl. I always tried to impress you with my daring feats. And I accomplished my deeds despite growing almost as tall as Cord in one year."

Ash snorted, which only added fuel to the burning fire of her displeasure.

"Honey, you're not that tall."

His endearment went a long way in appeasing her. "Did you just see Lady Charolois in the hallway?"

"No. I didn't see anyone."

"She just ran out of the door at the same time someone knocked me down."

"Someone knocked you down?" Ash pulled a pistol from beneath his waistcoat and scanned the room. He moved closer to her. "Are you hurt?"

"I'm fine, just shocked."

"Which way did he go?"

"I'm sure he left through the garden door when I was getting up from the floor."

"Did you recognize him?"

"No. When I was struggling to stand up, I heard the door open and saw Lady Charolois running out of the door."

"Let me take you to your room then I'll come back here to look around." Ash took her by the elbow and led her toward the door.

"I'm not going to my room. I'll go with you." She pulled away from his arm.

He took her arm again and led her to the hallway. "You're not going anywhere, but back to your room. You could've been hurt..."

She looked down the hallway and behind her before she whispered, "I'm fine. You said I could be part of this mission."

"I never said you could be exposed to danger."

"I want to help you, Ash." She edged closer to him. "I'll go to the drawing room and look for any gentleman who has wet or muddy shoes. And try to note any gentleman who is either missing or comes to the drawing room late. This will give you time to check out whether you can see any footprints by the garden door, but by the sound of the rain, I'm sure they'll be washed away by now."

"When did you come up with that plan?"

She brushed at the wrinkles on her dress. "Just now. It's the logical solution."

"I didn't want you to be involved. That was the reason we were supposed to meet here in the first place."

"You've already said all of this to me in London. I thought you changed your mind."

"I can't let anything happen to you. You know how much I care." He stepped closer to her and pushed one of her hanging tendrils behind her ear. He trailed his rough fingers down her throat, back and forth over her upper chest, then teased down into her cleavage. His touch caused shivery sensations to rush into her stomach and into her legs. His cat-like eyes were focused intensely on what he did with his fingers.

"I knew you cared, but you've never said." Her voice came out winded, breathless. "Why haven't you? I've been waiting."

"I wanted to finish this damn business before I declared myself. I didn't want the danger close to you, but now it's impossible."

"Not impossible." She stepped closer, her dress covering his pant legs. She wanted to crush herself against him and never let him go. "As long as I know you're mine. I can wait until this mission is over."

"I'm yours, Gwyneth." He wrapped her in his arms and brought her against his hot, hard body. His kiss wasn't demanding like their first. He gently pressed his lips to the corner of her mouth. He kissed her, light and easy, using his tongue, his teeth until they were both panting. "I need you, Gwyneth Beaumont, now and forever."

They lingered against each other in the hallway. She didn't want his kisses to stop.

"You need to go to the drawing room. And act as if nothing has occurred. Can you do that?"

She touched her shaking fingertips to her lips, her wide-eyed gaze locked on his. "I'm not sure I can hide my delight at finally sharing kisses with you, not after waiting for ten years."

Ash took her fingers and kissed each one. "Darling, I don't mean our kisses. I meant the conservatory."

"The conservatory?" She straightened the braid at her temple that had become loose when Ash had held the back of her head. She giggled. "I'm teasing. Of course I can focus on our job."

"Can you just be a guest? Not call attention to yourself by asking indiscreet questions."

"You know I can. I'm very observant and I'll inform you immediately of anything I notice that is suspicious. I won't put myself in any danger."

"Gwyneth, I couldn't bear if anything happened to you."

"I feel the same about you."

She kissed him. It was the first time she had ever initiated a kiss. She imitated the way Ash had traced his tongue on her lips and then thrust his tongue into her mouth.

"Desist. Don't torture me." Ash sounded like a winded racehorse. "We've got to get to work."

"I know, but I want you to remember that kiss while you're pursuing the tempting Lady Charolois. Remember you belong to me."

"She isn't a temptation to me. No other woman can be. Only you."

Ismay waited in the shadow of the kitchen garden, twisting her hands into a tight knot. She heard her husband's heavy footsteps before she saw him in the dim light.

"Where are the flowers?" Her French accent was stronger whenever she got stressed, but she needed the

Trumpet flowers to make the deadly potion. It was time.

"Lady Gwyneth Beaumont was in the conservatory. She almost caught me picking the flowers."

"Mon Dieu." Her hands went to her chest. "Did she see you, Francois?"

"No, I shoved her and ran out the garden door. I didn't see who she was meeting."

Her mind whirled with the possible difficulties in executing their plan. "Why would the lady be in the conservatory? Tryst? Or do you think she's the British agent we were warned about?"

Francois nervously ran his hands through his remaining hair. "I'm not sure, but remember her older brother is an agent. He has spent the last years in France."

"It was fortunate that we were privy to Fouche's private communications. How else would we've learned of the British infamy?"

"I don't believe this woman is an agent." He flicked his hand in the Gallic fashion and shook his head. "She's squeamish like all the British women."

Her husband shared her disgust of the British.

She stepped closer and whispered, "I can get the flowers later tonight when the house is asleep."

Francois loomed over her, his tone firm. "No. With suspicions aroused, I think we should wait. You need ten Trumpet flowers to prepare the poison and someone might notice if that many flowers are missing."

Cautious, Francois never acted on impulse. She tried to control the impatience in her voice. "But we've been planning this for a year. No one will suspect poison when the Prince Regent becomes ill. They will think he is having the same symptoms as his father, crazy as his father is."

He took her into his arms. Her husband wasn't fooled by her attempts to appear calm. "Our son will be revenged on Christmas, as you wish. You will be able to rest easy after the deed is done."

"I will never rest, but I'll have fulfilled my mother's duty to Andre."

He held her tightly against his chest. "We'll stay away from the conservatory for the next days. The

Prince Regent doesn't arrive until the end of the week."

She pushed out of his arms. Tired of waiting, she needed to finish—for Andre. "Did Lady Gwyneth report what happened in the conservatory to Lord Edworth?"

"No. She came to the drawing room and acted as if nothing untoward had happened." He studied her as he spoke. Francois was always watching and gauging her emotional state.

"Suspicious, don't you think? A proper lady would've fainted and had the entire house searching." She could barely contain her fervor as the day drew nearer, but she had to remain cautious and careful. "What about the other guests? Are there any who've spent a great deal of time in France?"

"Yes, Lord Ashworth. He also visited Lord Edworth last week," he said.

"Have Thomas watch him carefully. But we mustn't cause him to become guarded. If he becomes a problem, we'll deal with him. Holly berries are quite toxic and the same color as the Port that the gentlemen love to imbibe. Wouldn't that be a touching Christmas gift for our British spy?"

"Ismay, if the agent dies, the Prince Regent won't arrive."

"You're right, as always." She smiled at him, trying hard to keep the eagerness out of her voice. Francois worried if she got too excited. "I'll concoct the dose to make him sick enough to take him out of the spy game, but not enough to kill him."

CHAPTER SIX

Ash, with Lady Charolois on his arm, walked with the other houseguests down the winding path toward the woods. Today the house party would gather the greenery to decorate the manor in preparation for Christmas. The rain had finally stopped after two days, and everyone was relieved to be outside.

Dressed in a bright blue pelisse that matched her blue eyes, the lady leaned on him. Lady Charolois was quite a fetching little thing. She definitely didn't look the part of an assassination mastermind. His skills in threat assessment, honed by his years abroad, registered mixed messages about the lady's involvement.

Meanwhile, another lady caused his whole being to tighten into dangerous readiness, not due to clandestine plots, but due to male need and possession. Gwyneth, on Henley's arm, walked blithely along, smiling and chatting. Clearly, she was everyone's favorite. She played her part superbly, never showing any clue of her feelings for him or her role as an observer.

The crisp fresh air had added an attractive pink to her soft, smooth cheeks. Her pleasure in the event shone brightly on her animated face. Her dark eyes glowed with enthusiasm as her hearty laughter danced on the wind. His need and admiration for her had grown to ridiculous proportions. He wanted to meet her in a dark hallway, not to exchange information, but to fulfill his driving need to claim her as his own.

He suppressed his frustration and lust. This mission was simply torture, the worst he had ever encountered in his three years abroad. The love of his life acted available to every randy man in her vicinity and didn't every man know it. Her joy, her light, seemed to shine on all of them. He wanted to claim her exuberance for himself.

And to make matters worse, he was no further in solving the mystery of what possible threat awaited Prinny. He had no news from Cord on Aunt Euphemia's possible lead. Nothing out of the ordinary had occurred since Gwyneth had been knocked down. He had his footmen in the house watching Gwyneth, but with no clue to the threat, he didn't know how to intervene.

He would be relieved when Aunt Euphemia arrived. He definitely wanted the old girl on site when the Prince Regent arrived. With her years in France during the Reign of Terror, Aunt Euphemia could protect Gwyneth. He had to remain focused on His Majesty's safety and he couldn't be totally focused if he were worried about a threat against Gwyneth.

"She's quite a beautiful woman," Lady Charolois said.

He hadn't realized that he had allowed the conversation to dwindle.

"I beg your pardon."

"Oh, come, Lord Ashworth. The woman you and every gentleman can't stop staring at."

He had to pay closer attention to his job and stop acting like the ridiculous Henley, who hung on Gwyneth's every word.

"Lady Gwyneth? I've known her since she was a little girl. It's hard to imagine her as a grown woman."

What a bouncer. He wasn't having any difficulty with his "imagination." Every night he visualized exactly how and where Gwyneth had grown into luscious womanhood.

Lady Charolois' lips pursed in amusement. "I think Lord Henley is quite besotted."

Ash stiffened when he saw Henley put his arms around Gwyneth's waist and lift her over a fallen log. Her sunny laughter sprinkled the air.

He didn't want to discuss Gwyneth and Lord Henley. He was walking with the lady in hopes of detecting any clues that she might be connected to the plot against Prinny, if there even was a plot against the prince. "Are you acquainted with Lord Henley?"

"I've met the gentleman on occasion. The usual social rounds of the ton."

Ash's senses heightened as Lady Charolois' French inflection grew heavier and her hand tightened on his arm.

Ash didn't know what to think. If he weren't suspicious of her French connections, he'd have assumed that she was a woman scorned. "I've heard he's very close to making Lady Gwyneth an offer of marriage." God, he hated the spy game at this moment.

"I've heard the same thing," she said in a quiet voice.

Her eyes appeared to have tears, but he couldn't be sure if this was in response to the cold wind or genuine emotion. His years as a spy had taught him how calculating women could use their supposed frailty to their advantage.

He pretended not to notice Lady Charolois' distress. "Oh, look, they've found the holly. Shall we join them?"

Ash escorted the lady to the group standing in front of a giant holly tree.

Gwyneth's eyes were rounded in wonder, as if she had never seen such a spectacle. She gushed with emotion. "Now, it feels like Christmas."

He found himself, like everyone, drawn into Gwyneth's pure exuberance. Her eyes were untouched by the seediness of the world, and he wanted to keep her goodness protected.

He must have betrayed his feelings toward Gwyneth since Henley gave him a look that no male could misconstrue. With his body leaning toward Ash and his jaw jutted forward, Henley telegraphed his territorial rights over Gwyneth.

Every muscle in Ash's body tensed in response. He had never backed down from a fight and he would greatly enjoy planting a facer on Henley's glass jaw.

Gwyneth turned toward him. "Lord Ashworth, can you help gather the pine cones? The pine trees are ahead. The scent of pine is essential to a Christmas celebration, don't you agree, Lord Henley?" She released Henley's arm and walked toward Lady

Charolois. "Would you like to join us,
Lady Charolois?"

Gwyneth, the imp, had ruined the
fight. She hadn't missed the male
posturing. A hoyden herself, and
growing up with two brothers, she
recognized a brawl about to happen.

Gwyneth linked arms with Lady
Charolois. "You must tell me more
about your Christmas traditions in
France. Do you have Christmas
pudding?"

Henley eyed Ash warily.

"Shall we join the ladies?" Ash
realized he had acted like an ass,
allowing his feelings for Gwyneth to
interfere with the mission. "I've
always loved traipsing through the
woods gathering pine cones." Ash
added with sarcasm.

Henley laughed. "My sentiments
exactly."

Both ladies turned at the
gentleman's laughter. Gwyneth had
the nerve to wink at him when Henley
looked away.

Gwyneth circled the enormous pine
tree, gathering pinecones in her skirt.
Ash followed, leaving Henley to assist
Lady Charolois. He took her bounty

and made an enormous pile for the footmen to haul back to Edworth manor. The footmen would follow later with a wagon to collect the evergreens and the holly.

Satisfied with her pile, Gwyneth glowed in satisfaction. "Shall we go deeper into the woods to look for the elusive mistletoe?" Ash liked the way her voice lilted with excitement. She was a wood fairy, Artemis, the Greek goddess of the wilderness.

She took Ash's arm, forcing Henley to offer Lady Charolois his arm. "Did you know the mistletoe leaches nourishment by living on another tree? At our estate, mistletoe grows on a eucalyptus tree. I think we might have to walk quite a distance to find some. You gentleman will definitely need to do the climbing. As a girl, I always raced my older brothers, Gray and Cord, claim the mistletoe. If I weren't wearing these d...these clothes."

Ash tried to suppress his chuckle at Gwyneth's almost unladylike use of the word "damn."

"Lady Charolois, is something wrong?" Gwyneth touched the

woman's arm. "You look distressed. I hope my chattering hasn't upset you? This is my favorite time of year, and I do get carried away."

"No, Lady Gwyneth, I'm enjoying your reminiscing. I'm afraid I've worn the wrong boots for such a long walk in the woods." She lifted her dress to reveal a pair of denim half-boots.

"Oh, my. You're right. Those boots will be destroyed in the mud. We'll need to postpone our search for mistletoe to another day." Ash heard the disappointment in Gwyneth's voice.

"Oh, I would never make you alter your plans because of me. I'll return to the group. You must go ahead without me," Lady Charolois said.

Henley, a true English gentleman, stepped to the lady and offered his arm. "I'll escort you back to the group. We can help with the gathering of the greens."

Lady Charolois looked stunned by Henley's offer. Ash didn't miss the shift in Henley's shoulders to a protective stance and a look of concern. There was definitely something between those two, and Ash would bet his best curricle it had nothing to do with espionage.

"Lady Gwyneth, shall we continue our search for the mistletoe?"

Gwyneth took his arm and squeezed it tightly. It took all his control to maintain decorum. He whispered, "Watch yourself."

She gazed up at him. Her unabashed feelings reflected in her eyes for him to see. "Ash, it is so hard to keep up appearances when all I want to do is be with you during this wondrous season."

"Darling, I know. It's the same for me." Of course, she wanted to share the traditions of the holiday and all he thought about was her sharing his bed. "Not much longer and we'll have many Christmases ahead of us."

"I know. It's what sustains me."

"Gwyneth don't look at me like that, or I'll do something we both might regret."

"I won't regret whatever you want to do to me, Ash." Her voice got that husky tone that shot right down his spine into his groin. "Wait until I get you into the woods, away from everyone."

"You mean we're not going to look for mistletoe?" Her teasing voice had the same telling effect on his body parts.

"I think you might have competition for Henley's attention," Ash said.

"What?"

"Henley seems to be interested in Lady Charolois."

"Yes, the poor man. He doesn't realize he's in love with her."

Now it was his turn to be shocked. "What?"

"Yes, but that's not important. The important part is I'm not sure Lady Charolois has any connections to the threat against the Prince Regent. Except for seeing her flee the conservatory."

"What?" He asked.

"Ash, what is the matter with you?"

Nothing that a night with Gwyneth wouldn't cure. Who was he kidding? It was going to take a lifetime of nights to satiate himself with Gwyneth.

"I maneuvered the couple together so I could share my news."

Cord and Aunt Euphemia were correct. Gwyneth was skilled at subterfuge.

"Wait a minute. You weren't supposed to know about the threat against Prinny."

Gwyneth dropped his arm and he gave her the same look he'd given her in childhood when she was about to wallop him—once she'd punched him right in the nose. Of course, deservedly so—he had dunked her in the horse trough after she had interrupted him with the miller's widow. Her excuse was that she had come to rescue the woman when she heard the woman moaning as if in pain.

"It doesn't take an idiot to deduce that you're worried about the Prince Regent's safety at the house party— that you're looking for possible connections from some intelligence you got in London. Why can't you trust me?"

"I trust you. I just don't want you to be involved in anything dangerous."

Gwyneth rolled her dark, velvet eyes and stomped off down the narrow path. She walked quickly and he had to run to catch up with her.

"Look, there." She pointed to a large oak tree with the mistletoe hanging from a high branch.

She stood under the tree gazing up.

"You know what this means?" he asked.

She turned and stared at him.

He stepped toward her, crowding her against the tree. "I get to kiss you under the mistletoe."

Her eyes widened and her lips parted. She stood very still and waited.

He carefully undid the ribbon of her bonnet tied under her chin. His knuckles pressed against the beating pulse in her pale, white neck.

He teased her by pressing soft kisses on her cheeks, her nose, and then on her lips. Her lips were warm and soft, and he wanted to do so much to her.

She wrapped her arms around his neck. "Oh, Ash. I just melt when you kiss me."

She returned his kiss with her mouth open, her tongue darting in and out of his mouth. Lust roared through his body. He pressed her against the tree, his hard body rubbing against her inviting, womanly curves. He ran his hand along her pelisse, searching for skin to touch. He ground his erection into her body as his hands took her soft, ample breasts into his hands.

He held her fullness between his hands, squeezing them tight. He circled each nipple with his finger. She groaned and threw her head back. He was thinking about how he could take her, lift her skirts and push into her tight warmth.

"Don't stop, Ash. Don't stop."

Her words brought him back to reality. His hands shook, and he couldn't stop himself from teasing her nipples one last time before he dropped his hands. His erection throbbed against her soft thighs.

He leaned his head against her forehead, trying to catch his breath.

Gwyneth opened her eyes. "Why have you stopped?" Her voice was breathless, and he felt the little puffs of her moist breath against his cheek.

He started to laugh. She looked so rumpled and unhappy, and all he wanted to do was kiss her and make her happy in the way she begged him.

Indignant at his laughter, she tried to get him to release her, pushing against him.

It took all his willpower to release her. He kissed her lightly, trying to soothe both of their jangled nerves. "Gwyneth, we've got to stop because at any minute, others will join us. Have you considered that? And I don't want to take you the first time against a tree. Although the idea still appeals to me."

"Oh, Ash, me too." She ran her tongue along his lower lip sending burning flames down into his already hot body.

"Gwyneth, please. Remember you promised me you'd be discrete."

She stiffened in his arms and then straightened her spine. She patted at her hair now hanging from its hairpins. "You're right. I do have some interesting things to tell you."

He bent down and picked up her bonnet and handed it to her. He wanted to tie the ribbons, but she batted his hands away. "I've got to tell you what I've discovered. I spoke with the housekeeper about my love of plants and the conservatory. I asked her if anyone in the household or guests have been visiting the conservatory."

"It seems more of a question for the butler."

"Yes, you're right, but Brunton has only been with the household for six weeks and here's the interesting part. The chef is also new to the household. It has Mrs. Hudson in a fluster that Lord Edworth has hired new staff before the Prince Regent's visit."

"Interesting." Ash wasn't sure if there was anything of significance here. Staff moved between households all the time, but he did agree that it was suspicious. "Why were both the butler and cook replaced?"

"The older butler got a letter saying his mother had died in Northumberland. And Brunton appeared the next day saying that he was sent by an agency. I don't think Brunton's appearance would be that questionable if the cook hadn't become ill soon after Brunton arrived, and he just happened to know a cook who could replace her. Mrs. Hudson said Cook has been with the household for twenty years and never been sick."

"But Lady and Lord Edworth must have looked into their references before they hired them."

"According to Mrs. Hudson, Lady Edworth was so upset by the butler leaving before the royal visit, she isn't sure how carefully Brunton was checked."

"It may be nothing, but it's worth investigating."

"There's more. The cook is French. The housekeeper doesn't like her, so I'm not sure how much to believe, but she said the woman puts on airs—says she cooked for nobility and other esteemed personage in France."

Ash's instinct flared. "You've done well, Gwyneth. This is very helpful."

"And the most important part is that Mrs. Hudson said that she has seen the cook coming out of the conservatory."

"Wouldn't she need to go into the conservatory to get herbs and spices?"

"The herbs are grown in the kitchen garden, not in the conservatory," Gwyneth said.

"This mystery around the conservatory is baffling. I'm not sure what to make of it, except as a place that can be used for secret meetings."

"Did you find any footprints outside the conservatory?"

"Yes, there was one large print that hadn't been washed away from the rain."

"Anything else?"

"Only that the man who knocked you down has to be over two meters, which rules out most of the houseguests including Henley."

"Henley? Why do you think he'd knock me down?"

"You saw Lady Charolois running out. What if they are plotting together?"

"But why would he show interest in me if he were plotting with Lady Charolois?"

"To distract you. He knows Cord is your brother. Maybe he knows Cord's role in government."

"No, I don't believe it. Lord Henley is such a gentleman. I can't believe he could be a spy."

"But I'm a spy."

"But you're no gentleman." She rubbed herself against him. "A gentleman would never leave a lady wanting."

He held her tight against his body. His body flooded with lust. "What do you know about such things?" He kissed her deeply.

"I know enough." Her fingers wandered down the front of his breeches.

He grabbed her hand. "Gwyneth Elizabeth Beaumont. Stop. We need to get back."

He took her arm and directed her out of the woods.

Gwyneth protested. "But we didn't get any mistletoe."

"Another time," Ash said. "I need to talk with Lord Edworth about his staff."

"I'll plan to keep an eye on Cook and Brunton." Gwyneth added.

"What does that mean?" He didn't like the idea of her getting into trouble or drawing attention to herself.

"I'll visit with Mrs. Hudson, the housekeeper, again. Spend time in the conservatory. A lady interested in plants and household issues. Nothing to arouse suspicions."

"I don't want you to go into the conservatory alone. Take Amelia with you. And if you need help and can't find me, go to the stables. I've a man in the stables—Brinsley. He can be totally trusted."

"Ash, I want to be a help, but I wish we could be together."

"We will be soon, darling. This is my last mission, and then I'm done."

"It is dangerous for us to meet." Ismay stood against the outer wall of the still room, away from the kitchen windows.

"I had to take the risk. I've discovered the British agent. He was searching for my footprints outside the conservatory. Today he received a letter. I steamed it open. It was from Lord Rathbourne, and I'm sure it was in code," Francois said.

"Were you able to decipher the code?" Her husband had many talents. And Andre had been just like his father, clever, strong, and independent in his thinking.

"No, it is most likely a book cipher. I've no way of knowing which book they are using."

She wanted to rub her hands together in elation, but knew that Francois would disapprove of a show of strong feelings. "Who is the spy?"

"Lord Ashworth. As we suspected."

Her husband was methodical and logical. He would never jump to conclusions with everything at stake. "Thomas has followed him several times at night. He went to the stables in the rainstorm. I've inquired whether there were any problems with any of the horses and nothing has been reported. Lord Ashworth is our man."

Her heart rate accelerated with eagerness. Finally, she would get to act. Finally, she wouldn't be the victim. She would get revenge.

CHAPTER SEVEN

Gwyneth had planned her sleuthing well. She'd meet Cook early in the morning. At Rathbourne house, she met with Cook regularly to plans meals, but it would be unprecedented for a lady guest to have contact with the cook at another home.

She hadn't been able to share her plans with Ash last night. She had hoped to find a way to meet him for a review of their plans, but mainly so they could continue their kisses and the rest of the lovemaking that she was unacquainted with, but Ash was very experienced in. She was a very willing pupil.

Her plan had a few gaps, but she saw no way around the difficulties. She needed to meet the new cook and decide for herself if there was anything suspicious about her sudden appearance.

Gwyneth had already spoken with Lady Edworth who brushed aside the whole episode of new staff as inconvenient. The transition had gone smoothly—the French woman had proven to be an excellent cook and Brunton a good butler. Prinny would probably bring his own staff with him since fine cuisine was so important to him. Lady Edworth was also reassured that Mrs. Hudson was well satisfied with Cook's and Brunton's performance.

The trickiest part of the plan was to circumvent Brunton. Something about the man set all her intuition soaring and she trusted her instincts. Brunton and the staff would be occupied in the breakfast room at this time of morning. Mrs. Hudson would be occupied upstairs, directing the maids, so she should have time to sneak into the kitchen without alerting the other servants.

She planned to arrive unannounced. There was nothing anyone could say to a lady, but to allow her in the kitchen.

She followed the narrow hallway down the steps used only by the servants. She was well accustomed to the back stairs from Rathbourne house.

A startled footman stood at the bottom of the stairs, his muscular arms straining from the heavy tray of kippers. He averted his eyes once the shock of her appearance subsided.

Not sure what to do, he waited dumbfounded, the weighty tray in his arms.

"Good Morning...?" Gwyneth waited for the young man in his late teens to respond with his name.

"Thomas, ma'am."

"Your tray looks heavy, Thomas. I won't stop you."

"My Lady, may I help you?" His eyes narrowed and Gwyneth felt a sudden twinge of danger skirt along her spine.

"No, Thomas. I'm sure I can find my way to the kitchen. And I'm sure Brunton will not be happy if you don't deliver the kippers to the morning room."

"Yes, ma'am." His stare bordered on insolent and unsettling.

"Thank you, Thomas. That will be all." Gwyneth used her best hauteur. Growing up with Cord, she witnessed his methods of dealing with anyone who overstepped his place. She had never needed to use her lady-of-the-manor voice before today.

Thomas bowed his head and proceeded up the stairs.

Gwyneth followed the smells and the clatter of dishes to the kitchen down another long, narrow hallway.

As she entered the kitchen, the hectic noise stopped and all eyes turned toward her. Everyone paused and waited in the silence. One kitchen maid froze with her scrub brush in mid-air and stared with her mouth open.

"Good Morning." Gwyneth spoke in her most chirpy morning voice, the one she had used to irritate her brothers when they were tired.

All the kitchen staff bobbed their heads with bows and curtsies.

Gwyneth searched for Cook. At Rathbourne house, Cook always wore a crisp white apron. "I've come to speak to Cook."

"My Lady, Cook left to go over the menus with her ladyship."

Gwyneth was surprised that Lady Edworth was up this early, but with a house party of this size and the imminent visit of the Prince Regent, Lady Edworth was understandably busy with all the details.

Cook's absence gave Gwyneth the perfect opportunity to visit the still room. Mrs. Hudson's comment that Cook was the only one who used the conservatory was odd. Why would the cook not use her herbs from her still room?

Gwyneth had spent a great amount of time in both the still room and conservatory at Rathbourne house. She needed to study plants as part of a lady's role in household management, but it was also useful to know the treatments and remedies for the injuries and illnesses on an estate. But it was in the conservatory, which housed the exotic plants and the botanical discoveries of the new world that she spent the most of her time. Although not allowed to visit the other side of the world, she could imagine the glamorous worlds by studying the plants and the environment that nurtured them.

"I'm sorry to interrupt your work. Please continue. I'll walk outside in the kitchen garden." Gwyneth spoke again in her lady-of-the-manor voice, anticipating some reaction, since it was snowing outside and she wasn't dressed for the weather. But the servants bobbed their heads in acquiescence. She realized that the news of her visit to the kitchen and the garden would reach both Mrs. Hudson and Brunton before breakfast was finished.

She walked through the busy kitchen to the back doors, which she assumed would lead to the kitchen garden and a small shed used as the still room. The garden looked very similar to Rathbourne's winter garden—barren except for the winter greens. Cloth covered several of the less hearty herb bushes.

As Gwyneth suspected, the still room was a wooden shed, similar in size to the generous still room at Rathbourne house. Here was the heart of the kitchen with its herbs and spices. The strong scent of the dried lavender, sage, and thyme hanging from a trestle above filled the air. It was a comforting smell and brought back many memories of helping Mrs. Deighton, Rathbourne's housekeeper.

A long wooden table ran down the center of the room with drying racks on one entire wall. On shelves were pots, tubs, and labeled jars filled with the ground herbs. Edworth estate had a meticulously organized still room.

On one end of the table, holly branches and berries were piled. She recalled an experience from her childhood—a child in the village had eaten holly berries and had almost died. The berries were very tempting to children and animals alike.

Why would a well-organized still room have a poison on its table? Everyone knew of native poisons like nightshade and opium, and the care you needed to take in handling them.

Gwyneth carefully examined the area around the holly. Juice from the berry had stained the scrubbed wooden table. Her heart rate quickened as suspicions raced through her mind. She scanned the shelf to examine the several mortars and pestles for a sign of the red stain.

She found none, but the doubt wouldn't stop. She opened one cabinet that held the supplies, empty jars, twine, and the sticks for the garden. On the bottom shelf, behind a crock for storing the pickles was a mortar and pestle. And both were stained red.

A sickening heave of fear twisted in her stomach. She needed to find Ash. Could Cook be planning to poison the Prince Regent? She didn't have a reason for Cook's extraordinary behavior, but poisonous berries in the still room was not customary.

Gwyneth replaced the mortar and pestle. Her skin shivered with awareness. Suddenly she felt an overwhelming urge to get away from the still room and the disturbing evidence that she found.

She closed the door quietly as she walked outside. She had to find Ash before the morning hunt commenced, otherwise it would be all day before she'd be able to talk with him. She'd go through the kitchen garden to the back of the house and the courtyard.

She'd arouse inquiries if she came through the front door without a pelisse on. She hoped the French doors to the library weren't locked and that Lord Edworth wasn't in the library. With the hunt this morning, she doubted his lordship would be working on estate business.

She was in such a tizzy that she didn't take notice of the snow falling all around her, carpeting the hard, dark earth. She looked up to the skies. Snow for Christmas. She felt a rush of happiness and relief. If it snowed hard, then the Prince Regent wouldn't make it to the party and he wouldn't be in danger. Gwyneth hurried from the cold. She didn't want her red nose and cheeks to give away her secret enquiry.

CHAPTER EIGHT

Gwyneth hurried through the library to find an empty morning room. Had Ash already left for the hunt?

Brunton stood on duty next to the buffet table, supervising the footmen who delivered platters of eggs, sausage, and kippers, and removed the dirty dishes.

"My lady, may I prepare a plate for you?" Brunton's eyes trailed down the length of her, inspecting every detail. True to his training, he pretended not to notice or mention that the hem of her skirt was soaked from the snow.

"Thank you, Brunton. I'll serve myself. Have all the gentleman already left for the hunt?"

"Yes, my lady. Lord Edworth was very concerned by the weather so they started earlier than planned. Based upon how heavily the snow is falling, I believe the gentlemen will return before luncheon."

They both turned toward the long windows, bright from the heavy flurries of snow.

Drat, she had missed Ash. It probably didn't matter since they had two days before the Prince's arrival, but if Ash planned to contact Cord, he should send a messenger before the snow left them stranded. She needed to get dressed and ride out to join the hunt. Committed to her next plan of action, she hurried through her tea and toast.

As she climbed the horseshoe-shaped stairwell to the upper floors, she spotted Ash's valet, Worthy, moving toward the servant's stairs. He seemed harried and carried a basin covered with a cloth. Was Ash ill? She gripped the handrail tightly as if she could stop the panic shooting through her body.

In her most lady-like voice, she called loudly. "Worthy?"

The valet turned quickly. Shocked, he stood in place, frozen by her scandalous solecism.

She ran up the stairs, her skirts in hand—another breach of polite behavior. Her breathing became fast and she pressed her hand against her chest. Something was wrong with Ash. She remained fully aware of the dangerous game they were involved in and the necessity that she not draw attention to herself. But the halls were empty, the ladies still abed and the gentleman off on the hunt. And most importantly, Brunton remained in the morning room.

"My lady." Worthy was pale, and his hands trembled. "May I help you?"

"Is Lord Ashworth ill?"

The poor valet was flummoxed. He stared at her, unable to decide how best to respond.

"Please, Worthy. I'm a family friend and I'm very concerned."

"Yes, my lady. I've never seen him so ill, but he told me under no circumstances should I tell anyone."

Panic circled her like bees buzzing the nest. "Thank you for telling me, Worthy. I will see to the gentleman, myself." Gwyneth turned and walked quickly toward Ash's room. "But your lady…" She heard the valet following, but that didn't stop her from proceeding into Ash's room.

She wasn't prepared for the awful sight. Ash lay on his bed in a night robe. His color was white, his breathing shallow, and a fine mist of sweat moistened his brow.

"Ash." Her voice was filled with horror.

She felt his skin—cold and clammy. His pulse was irregular. Symptoms of possible poisoning. Could he have been the recipient of the holly berries?

"How long has he been like this, Worthy?"

"In the middle of the night, he became ill. Since this morning, he has uttered nothing, except your name. Last night he was adamant that I should tell no one of his illness. I was with his lordship in France and follow his directions explicitly…" Worthy let the implication hang.

"The master and I've been in some tight spots, but nothing this horrendous." Worthy's chin quivered. "I was about to go downstairs and speak with Brunton to call for the doctor."

Ash didn't want to alert anyone. If he'd realized that he'd been poisoned, he would've sent for a doctor. Burning red anger exploded in her. Ash had been poisoned and could've died with no one knowing.

"Lord Ashworth has been poisoned. And since you were with him in France, you know that his work requires secrecy. I'll need your help, but we mustn't alert anyone in the house since I don't know who we can trust."

"I'll do whatever I can for his lordship." His eyes were serious and understanding.

"We'll need plenty of warm water to give to his lordship. We must rid him of the poison." Anxiety caused Gwyneth's hands to tremble and her heart to flutter. She didn't know when he had consumed the poison and whether her treatment would be effective. "Can you summon my friend, Miss Bonnington? Tell her to come immediately here. Do not let her maid hear you."

He nodded his head in agreement.

"I know that will be tricky, but I need her and the water now. And leave the basin in the change room. We don't want anyone to know of his lordship's illness."

"Yes, my lady."

Worthy walked briskly out of the room, his shoulders set with determination for his mission.

Gwyneth knelt over Ash's body. "Ash, you aren't going to die. Now that you've finally declared yourself." Her voice broke with the words. She suppressed her feelings and the need to throw herself on Ash and weep. She couldn't give in to emotions. Ash needed her.

She'd force warm water down his throat to make him vomit the poison. She needed to prevent him from going further into a stupor. Worthy would go to the stable to get Brinsley, whom Ash had said she could trust. And Brinsley would get a message to Cord. She couldn't leave Ash, but she was stuck, uncertain what to do about the holly berries that she had found in the still room. She couldn't prove that Cook had prepared the potion. Anyone

could enter the still room and concoct
poison.

CHAPTER NINE

Fighting the poison in Ash's body continued through the day and into the early evening. Ash remained unresponsive to their ministrations, but Gwyneth refused to quit.

Inducing emesis with warm water had been repeated through the morning until Ash vomited only water and bile.

When he started to drift into a stupor, cold water was splashed onto his face and chest followed by Brinsley and Worthy forcing him to walk as they dragged him back and forth in the room, attempting to purge the poison from his body.

Brinsley had been a steady presence for Gwyneth, unwilling to give up on Ash. He had sent a coded message to Cord. One of the men in the stables had ridden out, but they all worried about him making it to London with the thick snow that covered the ground at Edworth.

Gwyneth focused on Ash who was showing some signs of improvement. His breathing was less shallow, his heartbeat was steady and some of his color had returned. He wasn't deathly white. She was exhausted and unable to differentiate between slumber and stupor any longer, but she had to maintain the regime.

Once more, she repeated the routine of the cold water on Ash's face for the umpteenth time. Ash opened his eyes. "What the hell?" He pushed against her so forcefully that Gwyneth almost fell off the bed.

"Ash!" Tears poured down her face as she ran her hand along his cheek. He was warm to touch—the deathlike chill had passed.

"Get off me, Worthy! His voice was tremulous, but he was conscious. He took a deep breath then closed his eyes. "Sleep... I want to sleep."

Gwyneth was no longer able to maintain her calm, stoic role. Painful sobs shook her body and made her unable to speak or breathe.

Brinsley proclaimed, "Thank God."

Amelia came to the side of the bed where Gwyneth was perched. "Gwyneth, he's going to be okay. You did an unbelievable job of nursing him.'"

Gwyneth turned and continued to cry on her friend's chest. "I'm so sorry, but I don't know what I'd have done if I'd lost him."

Worthy had tears in his eyes when he spoke to Gwyneth. "Lady Gwyneth, let me take over. You need to rest. I'll call you if there is any change."

Amelia pulled Gwyneth up from the bed. "Let me take you to my room. You can claim you have a headache. Your maid will believe your story since you look like hell."

Gwyneth burst into laughter, as Amelia had planned, but the hysterical laughter was mixed with painful gulps.

Amelia pinned back the falling hair from Gwyneth's chignon. "We must keep up appearances. I must dress for dinner."

Her friend had risen to the challenge. Amelia hardly acted shocked that the French cook had poisoned Ash because he was a spy. England was at war and everyone's perspectives had been altered. The English waited for the day Napoleon would invade their country.

"Yes, let's not forget about appearances," Brinsley said sarcastically.

"What would you know about good behavior, sir?"

For some reason Amelia and Brinsley had taken to each other in strong dislike. How two people who had just met this morning could have such strong feelings toward each other was difficult to comprehend.

"I must go down and pretend that nothing out of the ordinary has occurred and make excuses for Gwyneth's absence." Amelia smoothed the wrinkles on Gwyneth's crumpled muslin dress, but could do nothing about the wet spots from the tears.

Recognizing Amelia's worry by the way she fussed, Gwyneth took her friend's hand. "You're absolutely correct, Amelia. I haven't had time to think about dinner."

"You will rest in my room. I will tell your maid that I've designed a special dress for you tonight, and my maid will assist you in the dressing."

"It figures you'd spend your time on frivolous activities." Brinsley shook his head as he rolled his eyes upward.

Her amiable friend's voice turned hostile. "What is that supposed to mean, sir?"

Since everyone had been under incredible stress, Gwyneth ignored the outburst. "Will it be unusual if both Ash and I are missing from dinner?"

There was silence as everyone contemplated the implications of two absent dinner guests.

"It is acceptable to not participate in the day's activities, but everyone is expected to be at dinner. It will be noticed and remarked upon if you're both not at dinner," Amelia said.

"Ash has said that he planned to return to his own estate for the holiday. We could announce that he departed quickly because of the snow, but plans to return for the Prince Regent's arrival," Gwyneth said.

Brinsley nodded in agreement. "It will give us the time we need. And perhaps this is the right time for me to rejoin society."

"What?" Both Gwyneth and Amelia asked in strangled voices.

"Lord Jeremy Randolph Brinsley." The man built like an ox executed a bow worthy of the Queen's drawing room.

"You're not a stableman?" Amelia's bright violet eyes looked more dramatic against her pale white skin.

"I'm many things, my fair lady." He gave a roguish smile, accenting the dimple in his left cheek

"Lord Brinsley...your name is familiar." Amelia was staring at him. "You... ran off with your brother's fiancée."

"The estimable one." Lord Brinsley angled his head in an insolent fashion.

Amelia gasped. "Of all the nerve."

"Please, we don't have time for this." Gwyneth tried to take the edge off her voice, but she still sounded like a shrew.

"Lord Brinsley, your arrival will provide a distraction, but how will you explain your sudden uninvited appearance?"

"I'll ask Lord Edworth to understand that I'm in pursuit of a lady at the party. I've heard that Lady Charolois might be of interest to a gentleman with my reputation."

"Of course, she's perfect for you," Amelia said spitefully.

"I don't think it's a good plan to call attention to Lady Charolois since Ash suspects her of having ties to the French spies. I think you need to pick another lady."

"No respectable lady will go near him," Amelia sputtered.

"My reputation is a barrier for some ladies, but not all," he said in a low, seductive voice.

"Amelia?" Gwyneth raised her eyebrows in question. "You can pretend to be courting Amelia," Gwyneth said.

Both Lord Brinsley and Amelia answered at the same time. "Never."

"But that's the reason it will work. You obviously have had a fight and loathe each other, but Lord Brinsley has arrived to mend the wayward ways of love."

"Yes, it could work. In my pursuit of the lovely, respectable Miss Bonnington, I'll be privy to all goings on and it wouldn't be questioned if we devoted lovers steal private time in the conservatory. It will give me time to investigate the still room."

"And you can get messages to me through Amelia."

Amelia stood still, an unusual moment for her energetic friend.

Lord Brinsley moved closer to Amelia. A red blush immediately covered her pale face and chest. With her porcelain white skin, all her emotions were mirrored in her color changes.

"It will be all for show, all part of my work. You needn't look so frightened."

"I'm not frightened. And I'll do whatever Gwyneth needs me to do to help my country."

Gwyneth hugged Amelia. "Thank you. I knew you'd help."

CHAPTER TEN

With a candle in hand and dressed in her wool pelisse to hide her nightclothes, Gwyneth snuck along the quiet hallway toward Lady Charolois' room. This spy business was definitely exciting, but not particularly more challenging than sneaking into her brother's rooms to play tricks on them. She would never admit to being frightened, but the way her stomach fluttered and her knees quaked, she was telling herself one big whopper of a lie.

She hadn't shared with Brinsley or Amelia that she didn't plan to rest while they were at dinner. They would've tried to dissuade her from her search. They had no proof that Cook had poisoned Ash and they were no closer to discovering the threat against the Prince Regent who arrived tomorrow on Christmas Eve if the snow allowed. Ash was still too weak to pursue the mystery.

Gwyneth had waited to embark upon her late night mission until the servants had gone down to the kitchen for their dinners. She planned to look through the lady's belongings to see if there were any indications of her clandestine connections.

Shadows danced along the walls. She walked briskly, in fear that someone might see her. With the sound of footsteps behind her, she turned suddenly. Panic flared down her spine, causing her to shudder in fear. The flame of the candle on the pier table in the hallway flickered with her abrupt movement. She was scaring herself, getting melodramatic. She exhaled the breath she had been holding since she left her room. There was no one following her. Everyone was at dinner. The idea of helping Ash strengthened her resolve to continue down the hallway.

Lady Charolois' room was next. When Gwyneth turned the handle, the click echoed down the hallway and thundered in Gwyneth's ears. Her heart beat at breakneck speed.

The fire in the grate and the burning candle on the bedside stand created an eerie glow in the room. She closed the door behind her and walked toward the lady's wardrobe. She held the candle in her left hand as she carefully searched the closet. She opened the bottom drawers looking for letters. Tucked into one of the lady's boots, the same ones Lady Charolois had worn to gather the greens, was a pocket pistol. Interesting. Exceptional for a lady to have a pistol, but not proof that she was a collaborator.

Gwyneth found only that the lady owned an incredible amount of blue clothing. Lady Charolois definitely recognized that blue flattered her coloring and her eyes.

Gwyneth walked to the dressing table. She placed the candle on the table between the assortment of jars, glass bottles, and ceramic pots filled with a lady's beauty regime—a wonderful place to hide poisons. She sat on the stuffed lady's chair and picked up the largest jar and sniffed the contents.

The familiar smell of cherry laurel oil arrested her nose. Cherry laurel oil was used by ladies to make their skin supple and fresh, particularly around the eyes. Cherry laurel seeds were very poisonous. But Ash hadn't experienced the fever, rash or death that came from cherry laurel poisoning.

She examined a smaller jar before smelling the contents. She recognized the pungent scent immediately. Belladonna was highly poisonous and known to anyone who resided in the country. It was also used by ladies to dilate their pupils to give them the wide-eyed appearance that gentlemen considered attractive. Ash hadn't been poisoned with belladonna since he didn't exhibit the associated hallucinations or mania or death coma. This search hadn't uncovered anything questionable and she had no evidence against Lady Charolois except that the lady was a very vain woman.

Gwyneth examined and smelled the rest of the jars and containers—beeswax, rice powder, and evergreen bugloss, all used to make a lady's skin and lips beautiful, but nothing highly toxic.

At this point, she was forced to conclude that the conspirator hadn't planned to kill Ash, since there were more deadly poisons available. They had wanted to make him ill enough not to interrupt their real mission— the Prince Regent. If Lady Charolois had used either belladonna or cherry laurel, Ash would've died from the potent poison.

His symptoms matched poisoning by holly berries. She needed to get to the still room and retrieve the mortar and pestle as proof of deliberate sabotage.

Kneeling on the cold brick floor, Gwyneth searched in the dark for the mortar and pestle. She couldn't risk lighting a candle. The still room was easily seen from the kitchen windows. At this time of night, the kitchen was a hive of activity. The servants were cleaning up from the evening's dinner. She had avoided the kitchen by walking through the snow-covered garden.

She pushed against the heavy crock filled with pickles to probe for the mortar and pestle. The scent of dill hung in the air.

The clatter of dishes and bits of conversation from the kitchen were easily audible through the closed door. The chill running through her body heightened her awareness, making her highly-strung nerves tighten up.

Her fingers rubbed against the worn mortar and pestle. They hadn't been moved. Exultation rushed through her as she slid them out of their hiding place. Gathering the evidence of his poisoning was the best way to help Ash.

"Mon Dieu! What are you doing?"

Gwyneth startled and dropped the mortar on the ground. The harsh noise of the instrument hitting the brick floor reverberated in the silent room.

The muscular cook stood over her with a heavy candlestick in hand. Her face was contorted in rage, her eyes glazed with a frenetic frenzy.

Gwyneth's breath couldn't make it all the way down her lungs. She just stared at Cook, paralyzed by her adversary's violent stance.

"No one will stop me from killing the king's son."

And before Gwyneth could react, the woman swung the heavy candlestick above her head.

Gwyneth jerked away, but the solid metal struck squarely against the side of her head. The punishing impact propelled Gwyneth backward. Writhing in intense pain, bright lights flickered in front of her eyes before the murky black descended.

CHAPTER ELEVEN

Ash's head hurt like a son of bitch. He didn't remember over-indulging, but he had an agonizing headache, his mouth was dry and his body ached. This was worse than any hangover he had experienced during his days at Oxford. He couldn't stop the insistent burning and throbbing behind his eyes. The din from Worthy exacerbated the excruciating pain. He prayed to drift back into the empty black void and find peace.

Bright lights flashed, penetrated, despite his closed eyes. He was going to kill Worthy for opening the curtains.

"God damn it, man. Wake up. Gwyneth is missing."

Ash sat straight up, jolted awake. His heart thundered in his chest like a heavy drum with his sudden motion.

He stared at Brinsley, trying to comprehend what was happening. "Gwyneth?" He could barely speak. His voice was parched, as if he had been on a fortnight bender.

Worthy handed him a glass of water. He gulped down the water and pushed his legs from under the covers.

"You need to sip the water, sir. You don't want to be sick again."

Swinging his legs to the side of the bed made the room spin, and Ash felt as if he might vomit. He couldn't remember being ill. "What's happened to Gwyneth?"

"Amelia and I've searched her room and spoken with her maid. She told Lizzie that she was going to sleep, but her bed wasn't touched. And her pelisse is missing, as if she went on a journey."

Ash stood up, naked. His legs were rubbery and weak. He had a faint memory of being dragged. "Get my clothes. I must find her."

"But, sir, you're not recovered." Worthy stood next to Ash, expecting that he might fall and prepared to assist.

"Recovered from what?" Ash didn't have time for illness. His symptoms had disappeared as rage pulsing through his body at the idea of Gwyneth missing or hurt. He dressed in his smalls and pantaloons.

Brinsley stepped closer. "You were poisoned. We don't know by whom."

"What the hell—poisoned?" Ash slipped on his shirt. "How long have I been out of commission?"

"Less than a day, but Gwyneth was exhausted from taking care of you. Amelia took her to her room, expecting her maid to attend to her while you slept. Amelia came upstairs to check on Gwyneth and found her missing."

"Damnation. How long has it been since the maid saw Gwyneth?" Ash pulled on his boots.

"Since dinnertime, more than two hours ago."

"A two hour delay." Fear and anger swirled in a fomenting mess inside him. "We must act immediately. She could be captured or..." He couldn't bring himself to say the words.

"With the snow, her captors can't escape without leaving a trail. I've got men checking the grounds"

"Snow?" Ash asked.

"While you were out, at least two feet have fallen."

"Good." A moment of relief flowed through him. "That keeps our assailants trapped. Where have you searched in the house?"

"I didn't want to alert the staff, so I haven't searched the downstairs yet. I've searched the guest wing. Amelia is with Gwyneth's maid. I came here to get further instructions since I didn't know who can be trusted in the household."

Ash walked to his desk and pulled out his pistol. He tucked the weapon into his waistband. "My jacket, Worthy."

"Gwyneth was previously assaulted in the conservatory. I'm going to search there first. Find Lord Edworth and instruct him to say nothing to his staff or guests of Gwyneth's disappearance."

"You should start in the still room. Gwyneth discovered poisonous holly berries and a red-stained mortar and pestle hidden there. She concluded you were poisoned. If it weren't for her detection, we would've believed you had the grip and that assumption would've been deadly. She saved your life."

Bone-chilling fear flashed through his body in an instant. Gwyneth was in danger because she had tried to protect him. His heart smashed against his chest in deep crushing panic. He was used to risky situations but never involving the woman he loved. He would never let her out of his sight again once this horrific ordeal was over.

He walked briskly to the door, in command of his emotions, determined to find his beloved. "Brinsley, meet me in the still room after you have spoken with Lord Edworth. Draw no attention to yourself. We don't want to endanger Gwyneth by panicking her captors."

He turned back into the room. "Worthy, tell Amelia to keep the maid in Gwyneth's room. We don't want her going to the servant's hall and discussing Gwyneth's disappearance. Then go downstairs and see if you can learn anything from the servant's gossip."

Ash strode down the hallway. His thoughts centered on how he would punish any person who threatened or harmed Gwyneth. The calculating spy was no more; this was pure and simple revenge.

CHAPTER TWELVE

He grabbed his wife by her arms and held her tightly. "*Ne pas être dans son assiette*. You are not well. Let me take you away from here." He gestured to the giant manor behind them. They stood hidden next to an apple tree in the kitchen garden.

Her once beautiful face was contorted in pain. She would resist, but their survival depended on their escape. "We must leave."

She pulled away, sinking further into the snow. "I'll not. It must be on Christmas day." Her usual focused, cold control was cracking, giving way to the volatile emotions that drove her. "The king killed our son. We must kill his son."

She shivered, from her violent emotions or the bitter cold. "His Majesty will know the black pain of losing a child.... Never to escape the living torment."

He wanted to hold her and take away her suffering, but he was impotent to stop her grief.

If he had not eavesdropped on Fouche's private meetings, he would never have known that it was the English behind the assassination plot. But in rage and helplessness, he had listened at the door, heard of the fate of their only son.

He couldn't bear to lose his wife after losing Andre. If he didn't get her away, he'd lose her too.

Their lives had been normal until the monster Napoleon killed or exiled anyone who didn't fit into his plans to rule the world. Andre, a young Frenchman, with all the passions for Liberté, Égalité, and Fraternité was a sacrificial lamb in the unyielding grasp of Napoleon.

"We've got to leave before they find Lady Gwyneth." He reached for her, but again she shook him off. "We'll use our escape route and hide in London."

"We could kill her and hide her body until the Prince Regent arrives." Her voice was edging to the familiar rashness.

He couldn't let her descend into hysteria, not again.

"We'd be hanged." He used his soothing voice, the one that often helped her regain her control. "We must remain focused on our goal. With this snow, the Prince Regent may not be able to make the trip. We must leave soon or we'll be trapped."

"But it must be on Christmas." Her eyes had the same wild, tormented look as the first year after Andre's murder. "It must be just like Napoleon's Christmas assassination plot. Our sweet, innocent Andre, taken away as a killer, when the British King and his minions were the conspirators behind the plot to kill Napoleon."

If only he'd never told her about the British and their role in the plot, if only they had remained in France, if only Andre hadn't been killed.

CHAPTER THIRTEEN

Ash grasped the handrail as he descended the main staircase. He was wobbly, like a midshipman finding his sea legs. An iron will and determination to find Gwyneth kept him moving.

Ash didn't know the way to the Edworth's still room, but he assumed, like most estates, it was close to the kitchen garden. He would walk outside around to the back of the manor to avoid alerting his enemies.

Nodding to the footman at the door, he walked rapidly out into the night. The blast of cold air jolted him fully awake. A sudden memory of being doused with cold water flashed through his mind. What had Gwyneth been forced to do to save him?

His feelings for gentle Gwyneth, who had nursed him, were overwhelming. As a spy, he could trust or rely on no one. But uninhibited Gwyneth had broken down all his hard-earned, emotional barriers. She would not let him remain alone. A crack in his cold spy heart had splintered wide open for passionate Gwyneth.

He slogged through the drifts of heavy snow. His tall Hessians didn't stop the ice from soaking his breeches and socks. Alert in the quiet, he listened to the night sounds. Light from the house shone on the glistening white blanket.

As he plowed through the kitchen garden, he saw a large wooden structure next to the main house. His stomach rolled in alarm and rage over what he might find. He had first-hand experience of the enemy's violence, but he wasn't sure what he would do if they had harmed Gwyneth. He pulled out his pistol. Touching the familiar cold metal steadied his churning emotions. The thought of an injured Gwyneth crushed his usual calm, detached approach to a mission.

There were no sounds in the winter stillness other than his harsh breathing.

He waited by the door of the still room, assessing the danger. The snow had been trampled by more than one set of footprints. He walked the perimeter of the building, evaluating the risk. No noises came from the completely dark shed.

One window on the back side was blocked by snowdrifts piled high. His nerves were tight and battle-ready as his hand stayed steady on his pistol. He walked to the front of the building.

Out of the line of fire, he kicked the door open. His heart slammed hard against his chest as he waited for a fraction of a second before turning the corner and making himself vulnerable. With his finger on the trigger, he silently slipped into the room.

The only sound was a moan. Gwyneth?

Gwyneth lay in the shadows, a crumpled heap on the brick floor. His hands were shaking as he tucked his pistol into his breeches.

He knelt next to her, touching her face. "Gwyneth, darling."

She moaned with the touch of his exploring fingers. A large, wet welt jutted from the side of her forehead.

Fury rushed through his body. He'd make the bastard beg for mercy.

He quickly ran his hands over her cold face. "I've got to get you back to house. We've got to warm you up." His voice was tremulous, but talking aloud steadied him.

"I'm going to lift you. This will hurt." A silent Gwyneth chilled his heart and soul. He needed his chatty, enthusiastic Gwyneth.

Gingerly, he lifted her into his arms. She moaned again. A good sign that she wasn't unresponsive to the pain—an ominous sign in head injuries.

"You're a load, my girl." He kissed her temple as he pressed her against his chest, his heart expanding with unfamiliar feeling of tenderness for his intrepid woman.

As he trudged through the snow, he was aware that his enemies might be close by. He wasn't worried about protecting Gwyneth. He was primed, his muscles clenched, ready to kill anyone who might threaten them.

Hiding an injured Gwyneth from the household was going to be trickier. He walked to the back of the manor to go through the library's French doors. He hoped that the men had retired for the night. The library always had a fire blazing and was well lit.

"Ash." Brinsley moved quickly through the snow. His pistol was drawn.

At the sight of Gwyneth with blood on her face, Brinsley said, "Holy hell." He opened the doors to the library. "How badly is she hurt?"

"Some bastard smashed her on the head. She's got a nasty bump, but I'm more worried about how long she's been out in the cold."

Gwyneth moaned and Ash realized he had squeezed her tightly with the force of his explosive emotions.

"Darling, I'm sorry." He carried her toward the blazing fire.

"Ash?" Gwyneth opened her eyes and looked up into his.

His bitter, cynical spy heart melted with unwavering love. "Thank God."

Her voice was muted. Her face was pale and bruised, her thick black hair matted with blood, and she had never looked more beautiful.

"Brinsley, move the settee closer to the fire."

Gwyneth, in his arms, twisted to talk with Brinsley. "You must find the cook. She's out of her mind. She plans to kill the prince."

"No need to worry about that right now." Ash lowered her to the settee.

"Ash, they're going to kill the prince." She grabbed his arm as he was tucking a pillow under her head. "You've got to stop them."

Ash tenderly pushed back Gwyneth's hair to look more closely at her injury. "Brinsley, we need to get a doctor. Send for a footman."

Ash gently guided Gwyneth's shoulder. "Lie back down."

Gwyneth batted at Ash's hands. "I don't need a doctor. I'm fine. Amelia and Lizzie can attend to me. You need to find Cook. She is out of her mind, and I don't believe she plans to just bash the prince on the head like she did to me."

"That woman did this to you?" Ash suppressed his need for revenge. He couldn't beat the daylights out of a woman.

"She was crazed, insisting that I wouldn't stop them from killing the Prince Regent. Something about the king killing their son and them getting revenge, but why would the Cook want to kill the prince?"

"Brinsley, pull the rope so I can summon Amelia and Lizzie."

Brinsley walked to the fireplace and pulled the bell-cord.

Ash directed the footman to summon Amelia and Lizzie and to bring a basin of hot water. He walked back to Gwyneth and sat on the end of the settee. "Once we've got your wound cleaned, I'll carry you to your room and get you out of these wet clothes."

"I'm getting very toasty, Ash." Gwyneth's face was turning pink with the heat from the fire.

He opened her wet pelisse, exposing her lace night rail. When he saw the sexy, flimsy night gown she had worn under her pelisse, shock and lust made his voice loud and rough. "You don't have clothes on!"

Brinsley cleared his throat. "I'll wait for you outside..."

Once Brinsley closed the door, Ash demanded, "Why aren't you dressed?"

"I had to change into my night clothes so Lizzie wouldn't become suspicious."

"You went outside with no clothes on?"

"Ash, forget my clothes! You need to stop Cook before she escapes."

Ash shook himself as if he were in a bad dream. Gwyneth, almost naked, had wandered the grounds looking for spies. "When I get back, we're going to have a serious talk."

The sparkle returning to her dark eyes and her plush lips curving into a sexy smile told him that the minx knew exactly what she was doing to him. Because when he got her alone, he wouldn't be interested in talking.

He bent over her and kissed her tenderly. "Are you sure you don't need a doctor?"

"I'm fine. Go. I'll be here waiting for you after you've caught them."

He pressed her palm to his lips then walked toward the door.

"And don't you get hurt, James Henry Ashworth."

CHAPTER FOURTEEN

Ash braved the cold night. Falling snow shimmered in the star-filled evening. Torn between duty to his mission and concern for an injured Gwyneth, he was on edge, a tangle of extreme emotions. Most people were at home enjoying the holiday season, anticipating Christmas day, but he was forced to leave the woman he loved to pursue French spies. Battered, lying on the settee, Gwyneth, no melting debutante, had pushed him out the door to capture the conspirators. He smiled to himself. She was perfect—a perfect wife for a spy.

His need for revenge on Gwyneth's assailant wouldn't be satisfied—he wouldn't be able to achieve justice by pummeling the attacker since she was an old woman. But he'd certainly make sure she went to prison for a very long time.

Brinsley and four of the hearty stablemen, all military, stood huddled together. Two of the men held lanterns over Foster, a military scout, who was bent over the tracks leading into the woods.

"How many are there?" Ash asked.

"Only two. One is definitely a man. Those prints are much larger than the other set. I'd say a woman and a man." Foster would have no trouble tracking Cook and her conspirators. "Also, the tracks are relatively new."

"They might be planning to meet their associates." Ash looked at the grim, determined faces of his hand-selected soldiers. "Are you ready to find our French enemies?"

The men nodded their heads.

Foster, lantern in hand, went ahead of everyone. Ash, following Foster, led the armed men in single file into the heavy thicket of woods behind Edworth manor. Brinsley brought up the rear. "Douse the lanterns," Ash commanded.

They walked in silence, listening to the stirrings of the wind and a night owl on the hunt. The snow buffered the sounds, turning the woods and gardens into a hushed, silvery world.

Foster continued to follow the tracks until he came to a small clearing. He signaled Ash to come forward. "They rested here."

Ash looked at the snow and the jumble of random footprints. He trusted Foster's tracking experience. "Did more join them?"

"No, these are the same two sets of prints. "

Ash nodded. He signaled to his men to keep moving.

They walked deeper into the woods. The cold penetrated their feet and their exposed hands, gripping their guns. Alert to the danger of a possible trap, they ignored the cold as the least of their worries.

Ash heard a muffled sound, approaching footsteps. The hairs on the back of his neck stood on end. He raised one hand to signal the men to stop and remain silent. Foster pointed toward a clearing twenty yards ahead. Ash turned toward the line of men behind him and gestured for them to encircle the enemies.

He pointed to Brinsley to follow him and to Foster to fall back. He didn't want Foster in the line of fire.

With his gun pointed, he walked toward the sound. Brinsley followed behind. As he got closer to the clearing, he spotted the dark clothing between the trees. The snow was working to his advantage, providing a stark contrast.

In a hushed voice, he said to Brinsley, "Cover me. I want to make them believe I'm alone—draw out the others if they're hiding."

Brinsley gave a thumbs-up.

Discarding stealth, Ash allowed the heavy sound of his boots dragging through the snow and the sound of branches breaking under his feet.

Unceremoniously, Ash walked into the opening, where Brunton, the butler, pushed a middle-aged woman behind him. "She had nothing to do with it. It was me." He used his butler's authoritarian voice.

The tension coiled in Ash's body relaxed—the butler wasn't armed. Ash stepped closer to get a look at the woman, who was blocked from his view.

"No, Brunton." The woman shoved Brunton and stepped into the clearing. She raised a pistol that appeared too old to fire and aimed the damn gun right at Ash. Aimed at his heart, she pulled the hammer back. "One dead Englishman is better than none. For our French son."

"No, Ismay. No." Brunton grabbed her arm, causing her shot to go wild.

Ash dropped to the ground as a pistol shot shattered the silence. Brinsley had fired from behind a tree at close range. Unlike the woman's misfire, Brinsley's shot struck her in the side of the head. She dropped to the ground, her blood soaking into the white snow.

Brunton collapsed next to the woman. "No, God, no. I can't lose you."

She gasped, "Andre..."

"No, no. It wasn't supposed to end this way." Brunton held the limp body in his arms, sobbing. "I've lost them both...for nothing."

Ash bent down and felt for a pulse on the fallen woman. He lifted the broken butler by the arm. "Come on.

Let's get you both out of the cold. My men will carry your wife. She is still breathing."

Brunton took his coat off and wrapped it around his wife.

Brinsley lifted her easily into his arms, his face twisted in regret. "The doctor will look after her wound."

Watching Brunton's anguish for the woman he loved, Ash was consumed with a sudden need to get back to Gwyneth. He couldn't bear to waste another minute without her—he wanted to hold her tight against him forever.

EPILOGUE

Ash and Gwyneth waited in line to be presented to the Prince Regent at the Christmas Eve ball. The snow had melted enough to allow the prince to travel to Edworth Estate. In the last twenty-four hours, Gwyneth had been in her room on forced bed rest with no private moment with Ash to hear any details of the capture.

Gwyneth stood close to Ash, trying to keep her curiosity and voice subdued. "My instincts were right about Brunton, but why did he and Cook want to kill the prince?"

Ash bent down and spoke in a low voice. "Their son had been executed by Napoleon as a conspirator in the Christmas Assassination plot."

Ash's muscular body bent over her, gave Gwyneth a sense of privacy in the midst of the holiday revelers. "Christmas Plot?"

"French monarchists attempted to blow up Napoleon on his way to the opera. On Christmas day, they detonated a bomb, killing innocent bystanders, but sparing Napoleon."

She grasped his arm. "But why kill our prince?"

"Napoleon knew that the monarchists were behind the plot, but he used the bombing to justify purging his enemies. After he declared himself Emperor, he didn't want any memory of his past association with the Jacobins. He exiled hundreds and executed innocent men, all under the guise of responding to the threat against his life."

Gwyneth turned toward Lord Smithton and his wife who stood behind them and gave her most charming smile. She nodded towards the lady and then leaned against Ash as if sharing the latest on-dit in society. "I'm assuming the Metge's son was one of the executed?"

"Their son was a political agitator whose only crime was that he distributed pamphlets protesting

Napoleon as Emperor." Ash shook his head in disgust over the injustice. "His mother, overcome with grief, was convinced the British were behind the plot. She wanted revenge on King George by killing his son on Christmas day." Ash chose not to share the fact that the British had funneled the financial support to the French monarchists. He didn't want Gwyneth to be any more upset than she already was by the last days.

"What a tragedy." Gwyneth understood what happened to families when a child died. Her parents were never the same after her older brother died. None of them were. Gwyneth tightened her hold on Ash's arm. "The poor woman, I wish there was something we could do to help her."

Ash gently caressed Gwyneth's resting hand. "I'm sending them back to France, never to return to England. I've seen too much suffering of innocent people caught in Napoleon's machinations. Brunton will care for his wife in his childhood village."

"Oh, Ash. What an amazing Christmas gesture of peace." She wanted to kiss Ash right in front of the

Prince Regent and would've if Lord Edworth's hadn't finished his long exchange.

They stepped forward to the enormous chair bearing the hefty Prince Regent. "Your highness, may I present Lady Gwyneth Beaumont?" Ash spoke in a formal, proper voice that she had never heard before.

Gwyneth had been presented to Queen Charlotte, but she had never met the Prince. She had heard all the rumors about Prinny and his excesses. By the harsh lines around his eyes and petulant mouth, the gossips had not exaggerated.

"Rathbourne's sister?" She heard the Prince query one of his attendants.

Gwyneth curtsied deeply in court fashion. She raised her head slightly to smile at the Prince Regent.

Prinny's eyes drifted downward, settling upon her décolletage. She was dressed in her pièce de résistance—the red velvet Christmas dress, designed to seduce Ash.

Not surprised by the Prince's usual lecherous behavior, Gwyneth was tempted to roll her eyes at Ash until she saw that Ash's soft eyes had turned dark and flinty and his body was clenched. Ash looked ready to plant a facer on the prince whose life he had just saved. Not that anyone would acknowledge or mention the assassination attempt.

Gwyneth hastily arose as Ash drew her to his side. "May you be the first to know, Your Majesty, that Lady Gwyneth has made me the happiest of men and has accepted my offer of marriage."

With his sagging jowls and his little beady eyes, the prince had the appearance of an enormous sea creature. He continued to stare at Gwyneth in the most intrusive manner, as if she were a treat he wished to devour. She could feel Ash's body tighten, ready to spring into action. She couldn't allow Ash to do anything rash, but she was unsure how to prevent such a disaster.

The prince guffawed. His rotund belly shook with laughter. "Nice work, Ashworth. The lady appears to be more than satisfying for a man of your position." The prince patted his sweaty face with a handkerchief as he continued to chuckle.

Ash's entire body remained taut, his hands fisted behind him. He bowed curtly and then led her toward the open doors.

Ash kept a possessive hand on her back. She could feel his warmth close to her exposed skin.

"Lord, spare me," Ash growled. "Of all the insufferable."

The reality of royalty was tiresome for an honorable man like Ash who had sacrificed years in service, only to be confronted with the profligacy of the Prince.

Ash took her arm as they walked through the crowded ballroom to an unknown destination. The gaiety of the holiday, scent of the pine boughs, and beeswax candles were in stark contrast to the tensions of the last two days when they had been assaulted, poisoned and set upon.

Not one to dwell on the negative, Gwyneth clasped Ash's arm. It was Christmas Eve and she was going to rejoice in the hope and joy of the season. She resolved not to allow the last days to spoil their first holiday together.

"It's almost Christmas. We must look for the Star of Bethlehem. Let's go outside through the library doors where it is private, but we must get back in time for the carolers. I love the singing."

Hopeful for the future and heartened by Ash's compassionate response to the Metges, she started to sing. "God Rest Ye Merry Gentlemen."

She stopped suddenly as they turned the corner. "It's Amelia...and Lord Brinsley."

Ahead, under the mistletoe, in a fervid embrace, stood Amelia and Lord Brinsley.

"They seem to be working out their differences." Ash chuckled.

"But Amelia loathes him."

"She has a funny way of showing her dislike."

Lord Brinsley's hands were wandering in places no lady should allow in public. Gwyneth was having difficulty not watching.

"Let's go to the library, shall we?" Ash's tone was wolfish and promising.

Anticipation danced along her skin as Ash took her down another corridor to the library.

Alone in the empty library, Ash's damp mouth moved over her, leaving a tingling trail from her throat to her collarbone, to the sensitive hollow of her shoulder. "I'm not going to want to go outside now that I've got you alone in the library. Especially in that dress. It was designed to drive men crazy. I thought Prinny was going to go into heart spasms."

The path of Ash's wet, hot mouth on her throat, arms and chest caught her body on fire. The memory of Ash's passionate reaction to her night rail the previous night made her shaky behind her knees. Suddenly she could barely stand with the overwhelming sensations Ash wrought from her body. She melted against him. "I chose this dress to drive only one man crazy—you, Ash, only you."

Sharing breath with him, she was drowning with the intimacy. "Oh, Ash."

"I haven't asked you formally, but, now that I told Prinny, you have no choice. You'll have to marry me."

The sexy command made her gasp—which was just the opportunity he wanted. His mouth nudged hers open more as he brought her into the solid cradle of his big, hard body. He sank his tongue, tasting her more deeply.

After long moments of pleasurable activity, Ash held her away from his body. "We must stop. Anyone can find us. You're going to be my wife. Besides, Cord actually might kill me."

The mention of her brother startled Gwyneth from her sensual haze.

Ash walked toward the French doors. "Come on, Gwyneth. I'm hanging on the edge here. Let's go outside to cool down and look at the stars."

"Oh, yes. It's Christmas Eve and like the three wise men, we have to look for the Star of Bethlehem."

Ash wrapped his arm around her as they stood together staring into the dark, clear night. Overhead was a bright shining star.

"There it is! The Star of Bethlehem. The promise of love and peace to come."

Ash looked down on her, his eyes filled with warmth and tenderness. "You're my Star of Bethlehem, Gwyneth. You're my promise. And I promise to love you always."

"As I do you, Ash. You're my star of hope and love."

"Your light outshines any star, my love."

ABOUT THE AUTHOR

Descended from a long line of storytellers, Jacki spins adventures filled with mystery, healing and romance.

Jacki's love affair with the arts began at a young age and inspired her to train as a jazz singer and dancer. She has performed many acting roles with Seattle Opera Company and Pacific Northwest Ballet.

Her travels to London and Paris ignited a deep-seated passion to write the romantic, regency The Code

Breaker Series. Jacki is certain she spent at least one lifetime dancing in the Moulin Rouge.

Jacki has set her Grayce Walters Mystery Series in Seattle, her long-time home. The city's unique and colorful locations are a backdrop for her romantic mystery.

Although writing now fills much of her day, she continues to volunteer for Seattle's Ballet and Opera Companies and leads children's tours of Pike Street Market. Her volunteer work with Seattle's homeless shelters influenced one of her main characters in An Inner Fire and Women Under Fire.

Jacki's two Golden Labs, Gus and Talley, were her constant companions. Their years of devotion and intuition inspired her to write both dogs as heroes in each series.

A geek at heart, Jacki loves superhero movies--a hero's battle against insurmountable odds. But her heroines don't have to wear a unitard to fight injustice and battle for the underdog.

Look for more heart-pounding adventure, intrigue, and romance in A

Code of the Heart—A Regency Novella, next in the Code Breaker Series, to be released on Valentine's Day 2015.

To learn more about Jacki and her books and to be the first to hear about giveaways join her newsletter found on her website: **www.jackidelecki.com.**

Follow her on FB—Jacki Delecki Twitter @jackidelecki.